SUMMER AT DORNE

Summer at Dorne

by

Mira Stables

Dales Large Print Books
Long Preston, North Yorkshire,
BD23 4ND, England.

British Library Cataloguing in Publication Data.

Stables, Mira
Summer at Dorne.

A catalogue record of this book is available from the British Library

ISBN 1-84262-322-2 pbk

First published in Great Britain in 1977 by Robert Hale Ltd.

Published in Large Print 2004 by arrangement with Robert Hale Ltd.

Dales Large Print is an imprint of Library Magna Books Ltd.

Printed and bound in Great Britain by
T.J. (International) Ltd., Cornwall, PL28 8RW

For Mabel

SUMMER AT DORNE

When Dominic pulled an unconscious girl out of the quarry pool he had never heard the old saying that holds a rescuer responsible for the life he has saved. Certainly Chantal needed help in the difficulties and dangers that faced her, but she was of an independent turn of mind and had little liking for the reluctant support of a self-confessed misogynist. A summer spent in the idyllic setting of the ancient castle of Dorne was to teach both of them a truer sense of values.

One

'My dear Shan! You will permit me to say that, in the circumstances, your scruples are a little absurd.'

The girl eyed him steadily. 'I am not your dear Shan,' she said quietly. 'If you wish me to listen to your remarks, you will address me with due formality. I may have to submit to your odious society, but "Shan" was Papa's name for me and I will not have it soiled by your lips. As for my scruples, you may accept them as unshakeable. It will save you considerable loss of face in the end.'

The Honourable Giffard Delaney, second son of the new Earl of Hilsborough, sought to ease a too-short neck in a too-high stock and smiled thinly at his cousin. 'As you wish, my dear,' he conceded, affecting indifference. 'Shall I call you Cousin? Or must I address you as Milady, since we are but second cousins after all? In any case it is of little account, since by the end of the week you will be my bride. And then I shall address you as I choose – *and* take steps to deal with your curst superior ways. I make no doubt that within a month you will be as sweetly docile a wife as a man could desire. I quite look forward to the taming process. I always enjoyed breaking a filly of spirit.'

Chantal had seen her cousin's ways with his cattle; had heard stories of his dealings with any wench upon whom his capricious fancy chanced to fall. She knew the mercy she might expect at his hands. But her father's blood was quick and proud within her. Not by the quiver of an eyelash did she betray the sick fear that surged in her breast.

'You are mightily confident, sir, to bespeak me so,' she told him coldly.

He laughed. 'And with good cause,' he told her merrily. '*My* father wholeheartedly approves the match. *Yours* made you a very attractive bride when he endowed you with all the unentailed estate in addition to his private fortune. I doubt if the money alone would have been sufficient to appeal to me,' he went on judicially, 'and since my brother must inherit the earldom I must do as best I can for myself. I have a fancy to be a landed gentleman. With your acknowledged physical charms to sweeten the bargain' – he bowed mockingly – 'it was irresistible.'

'And I am to have no choice in the

matter?' she wondered scornfully.

'Not now, my dear. Six months ago, perhaps. But not now. It is all settled. As a gentleman I stand too far committed to be able to withdraw in honour.'

He smiled, as at some private joke. There was something unpleasantly convincing in his manner. She did not see how she could be forced into marrying him against her will, but anxiety was growing within her. Somehow, despite her revulsion, she must try to discover what was in his mind. If she could draw him out – his conceit was his weak point – persuade him to display his cleverness to the helpless victim, she might learn how to escape the trap that threatened to close upon her.

'Indeed, sir, how may that be?' she enquired innocently.

He *did* hesitate. But the temptation to boast, to repay her contumelious attitude by showing her how her own behaviour had played into his hands, was more than he could resist.

'You were always such an odd creature,' he reminded her maliciously. 'Oh – never flouting the bounds of propriety, of course, but definitely eccentric – outré. To the only child of a wealthy earl, much is forgiven. But it is not forgotten. Those occasions when you made a mockery of rigid conventionality must have rankled in many a dowager's bosom. A pity you cannot hear them now. "Poor dear Lady Chantal," they murmur in the boudoirs and wherever the chaperones gather. "Such a tragedy! But, not really surprising. One always felt that she was not quite – er – normal. It is natural enough that the balance of her mind should have been finally overset by the horrid circumstances of her Papa's death, for whatever you may say to her discredit, Lucinda, she was perfectly devoted to him. Oh no! No hope at all, or so I am informed. A number of her friends have driven down to Delaney Court to visit her, but she receives no one. John Summerhayes saw her riding out in the grounds and said she looked well enough, but I believe they keep a careful guard on her. A grave responsibility, but one really could not endure the thought of the poor girl shut up in Bedlam. The physicians say that she is harmless so long as she lives very secluded in the country. She is very fortunate that her relatives are so kindly disposed. Not every man would have the patience to deal so tenderly with an idiot girl."'

He had mimicked to perfection the acid-sweet tones of one of her bitterest critics. She was left in no doubt that this was the tale that had been put about. Exactly the kind of tale that society would love, and knowing her cousin she had no doubt that it had been skilfully done. The grave face, the deep sigh; the half sentence bitten off just a word too late. And as regards her own conduct he had spoken truly enough. With no mother to guide and advise her and a father whose pride was in her courage and honesty rather than in decorous behaviour, she had ridden too high, and many would be happy to see her brought down.

It had been foolish, too, to seek shelter here at the Court when she had been so shockingly bereaved, though at the time it had seemed the natural thing to do. The Court was her home, the new Earl her father's cousin and her own nearest relative. Who could have dreamed that so simple and instinctive an action would breed such trouble? For that she was in very deep trouble she no longer doubted. Her cousin's disclosures only served to link and explain a long series of puzzling circumstances that had come to light during the past weeks. Ever since, in fact, she had begun to emerge from the shock of hearing of her father's death. Small things in themselves, yet mounting to a formidable total when taken together. It had seemed reasonable enough that the new Earl should have pensioned off Wagstaffe, her father's old butler, for he was sadly frail, and the grief of losing his beloved master had born heavily upon him. But it was odd that Wagstaffe had never come to bid her goodbye, and odder still that no one seemed to know where he had gone. Buried in her own grief – a grief that Cousin Giffard, in especial, was at some pains to keep alive by maladroit references to the more distressing aspects of her father's death – she had paid little heed when one by one the older members of the household staff were replaced by newcomers. She had Hepsie, her father's nurse, who had mothered her in childhood, maided her in girlhood, and who now remained her sole bulwark against the horrible fantasies that invaded her dreams and sapped her love of living.

She saw now, all too clearly, how she had delivered herself into the hands of her scheming cousin. He it was who had broken to her the full tale of her father's end; the small advance party set upon by savage tribesmen; the brave resistance against overwhelming odds; the inevitable end, with torture, mutilation and death for the man she had so dearly loved. Openly he had described unimaginable horrors, on the pretext that she, with her courage and her love of the truth, would prefer to know the whole. Small wonder that she had suffered for weeks from hideous nightmares and wakened screaming and hysterical. Easy enough, on that evidence, to put about a rumour that her mind was unhinged by her sufferings; to keep visitors from her lest they discovered the truth. And here, again, she had helped them by refusing to see even her most intimate friends during those early weeks. She recalled now, penitently, her own bitter remarks to Hepsie on the fickleness of human affection when the weeks had become months and still her former friends stayed away.

It was Hepsie's illness that roused her at last from the utter selfishness of her absorption. Since the tragedy the old woman had occupied a little slip of a room opening off Chantal's. The girl had only to call and Hepsie would be there. But there came a night when the call went unanswered, and Chantal, going in to investigate, had found the old woman sunk in a slumber so deep that it seemed to approach unconsciousness. It was then that, for the first time, she took note of the sunken cheeks, the yellowing skin and the colourless lips and realised that something was gravely wrong. Hepsie, struggling back to painful consciousness, did not deny it. She had consulted the doctor a year past, when the master first went off to Afghanistan. It was already too late. She had a canker lump in her breast and there was nothing to be done. The doctor had given her syrup of poppies to take when the pain was bad, and tonight she had taken a dose rather larger than usual. Which was why her ladyship had had difficulty in rousing her. Her only regret was that when death called her she must leave her charge unprotected. Otherwise she would be 'main glad to go.'

Forgetting her apathy in the need to tend Hepsie, sending a message to summon the doctor, arranging for tempting and nourishing food to be specially prepared for the sick woman, Chantal had suddenly awakened to the fact that she was practically alone among strangers. Even the doctor was new to the district. And everyone had treated her with a careful respect which she had ascribed to her mourning state. She realised now that it had probably had a very different origin.

'That was cleverly thought of,' she told her cousin. 'And I can see that there would be plenty of people all too willing to believe. But I do not understand how you expect it to forward your marriage plans.'

The compliment, trivial as it was, tickled his vanity. He was happy to tell her just what he had in mind for her. 'It accounts for the ceremony being conducted in private,' he explained. 'A bride of your social standing would naturally be expected to have a fine society wedding, but since you are so reluctant a bride, my father and I regret that we must deprive you of this pleasure. It would give you far too many opportunities of proclaiming your wrongs. But a bride who is touched in the upper works is a very different matter. We are held to have shown the greatest delicacy in our arrangements – indeed I understand that one or two ladies have been heard to express admiration for the nobility with which I am sacrificing my bachelor status in order that I can care for my poor little idiot cousin.' He giggled at the thought.

Chantal kept a firm hold on her temper. She must make the most of this communicative mood. 'But why put yourself to the pains of marrying me?' she said, wrinkling her brow as one genuinely puzzled. 'If you could have me pronounced insane, surely your father, as my guardian, would have charge of my estate?'

'Because the trick won't hold for ever,' he told her frankly. 'We've got rid of everyone down here who might know it for a hum, and fobbed off your friends from Town for the time being. But we can't keep you a close prisoner for ever. Sooner or later someone is going to turn up who will recognise that you're as sane as the next person. So by that time we'll have you safely tied up in matrimony, my dear, and no one will be more delighted at your complete recovery than your devoted husband, while all the world will declare that the miracle has been wrought by love.'

'It's an affecting tale,' she said drily. There would be no more to be got out of him. Already suspicion was again alight in the close-set eyes, a faint frown creased the white brow. She shuddered with distaste. The Honourable Giffard passed for a handsome young man, save that he was, perhaps, a trifle on the plump side. His close curling dark hair and the smooth, thick white skin had moved some of his admirers to vow that he had something of a foreign air – Greek, or Italian, perhaps. He reminded his cousin of nothing so much as the unsavoury creatures that stir to pallid life when a stone is overturned. 'It's a pity it will never be told. I repeat, sir, that nothing will persuade me to marry you.'

His mood changed with a vengeance. 'Who spoke of persuasion?' he said softly. 'If that is still your temper, my pretty love, to whom will you turn for help? You cannot leave the grounds. All the servants have been warned of the danger of letting you stray abroad; told just how pitiful and convincing you can be in your protestations. Who do you think they will believe? You have enquired once or twice about my father's absence. I did not see fit to answer you in detail at the time, not wishing to provoke one of your tantrums. He has gone to bring the clergyman who is to marry us. Oh yes! A genuine clergyman. No mock marriage for us. He is wholly devoted to my father's interest, being in fact his natural son, though this he does not know, and grateful for the education and training that enable him to support himself. He had the misfortune to contract the measles while sick visiting in his first parish, and as a result he is completely deaf. My father found him a post as librarian to some scholar recluse. Our pathetic story has been explained to him in writing and he has expressed his willingness to oblige Papa by emerging from his seclusion to marry us. How will you explain your predicament to him? Even if your mouthings and gesticulations alarm him, it will be but a matter of postponing the ceremony. He will be told that you are subject to fits at certain phases of the moon. And I, my love,' his voice rose in pleasurable anticipation, 'shall have the pleasant duty of bringing you to a proper state of submission. After a week spent in my apartments, I do not think you will lightly reject a second opportunity of being respectably married.'

She studied him with an oddly dispassionate gaze. Since her suspicions had been aroused they had burgeoned rapidly. It was no more than she had expected. As she gazed, his lips parted and the tip of his tongue was passed lingeringly over them. She sickened. The unconscious betrayal of that small gesture was more disgusting than his boastful words.

She said fiercely, 'I had rather throw myself in the lake.' And heard a servant's voice announce behind her, 'Luncheon is served in the morning room, sir. Shall I set covers for her ladyship?'

It did not need the triumphant gloating on her cousin's face to confirm the suspicion that her rash remark had been overhead and would go to confirm the story that she was mentally unhinged. She knew, too, what would come next. This was a recent trick – to keep her short of food. She had thought it designed to lower her physical resistance, but possibly it was also meant to further the impression that she was under medical supervision. She vaguely recollected reading in some journal or other that a low diet was recommended when the brain was thought to be affected. And here it came.

'Lady Chantal is not feeling quite the thing. She prefers to lunch in her own apartments. See that a light meal is sent up to her.'

She knew what she would find, as she slowly climbed the stairs to her room, revolving plans for escape, each in turn to be dismissed as impractical. The 'light meal' had been served to her on a number of occasions. At first, worried for Hepsie and lacking appetite she had paid little heed. But it seemed as though, while Hepsie's life flickered and faded towards its close, the eager young life in Chantal clamoured for survival. The meal – it might be a glass of milk and a slice of delicately thin bread and butter, or a cup of thin broth and a rusk – became a penance to be avoided if dignity permitted. The food was insufficient for an elderly invalid, let alone a healthy young woman.

At least, so far, they had brought food for Hepsie. At times the old nurse would seem a little better. There would be a temporary easing of her pain, and though she was growing very feeble her mind was perfectly clear. Sometimes she fancied her meals, at others she merely pecked at the food. On several occasions Chantal had hastily devoured the cooling remnants before putting the tray out. Once or twice Hepsie had nearly caught her doing it. Now, today, had come the threat of stopping the doctor's visits to Hepsie and the supply of medicine that was needed to allay the worst of her pain. It was this urgency that had made Chantal seek an interview with her cousin. And small good she had got of it, unless to have her worst suspicions confirmed could be counted a good.

Hepsie was up and dressed with her customary neatness, though heaven knew at what cost in physical anguish. She looked up placidly enough from her seat beside the fire in Chantal's room.

'And what's amiss with *you*, that you don't fancy your victuals?' she enquired in a voice that was little more than a thread, and nodded in the direction of the tray that had just been brought in.

One glance was enough. On the small table at the invalid's side stood her own empty tray, her meal obviously enjoyed today. Beside it stood a cup of broth, carefully wrapped and covered to keep it warm, not even so much as a rusk to keep it company. Chantal had endured a trying interview. She was frightened and hungry. The sight of that mockery of a meal was the last straw. She burst into tears and subsided on the rug at Hepsie's feet, her face buried in that comforting lap as she sobbed out her woe and desperation.

Hepsie was no fool. Already she had a strong inkling of the true state of affairs, though Chantal had done her best to keep her in ignorance. Now the girl's defences were down. She had no one but Hepsie to confide in. It needed but a few well-directed questions and the whole tale came tumbling out.

There was a long silence when it was done. Then Hepsie said slowly, 'You'll have to get away. I knew he was a wicked one but I never dreamed how bad. And to think he'd drag *you* down into the mire with his scheming. Well – no doubt the Almighty will punish him in His own good time, but we'll not dare wait for that.'

Chantal said curiously, 'You knew he was wicked? I never liked him, but I confess I never suspected him of such villainy as he has shown.'

''Twasn't my place to speak of it, but it was always there plain to be seen. I've heard tell he laughed when Mary Rogers drowned herself and her poor mother followed her to the grave. Wanted their cottage for a summer house or a Folly or some such whim.'

Chantal stared. She had forgotten Mary, though perhaps the memory had been dimly in her mind when she had spoken of throwing herself into the lake. Mary had only been fourteen. 'But surely it was not he who' – she began, and broke off in contemplation of a cold-hearted cruelty almost beyond belief.

'Was responsible?' finished Hepsie. 'No. I doubt poor little Mary was beneath his touch. By all accounts it was that nasty sneaking London valet of his that was responsible. And not every girl would have taken her shame to heart like Mary did. But she and her mother were as proud as the Delaneys in their own way. Proud of being freeholders and of being honest folk who paid their way and asked no charity. But talking pays no toll. Mary's dead and gone and beyond further hurt. It's how to get you to safety that we've to think about.'

And that seemed to be an impossibility. It was easy enough to decide that Chantal should make her way to London and put herself under the protection of her other guardian, her father's attorney and friend, Roger Dickensen. Between them they had more than sufficient money for such a journey, and it would be better to go to a man of law who was accustomed to sifting evidence rather than to friends who might have been gulled by cunning lies. But how could she bring herself to desert Hepsie, who certainly could not stand such a journey, and how was she to escape from the Court?

'As for leaving me,' said Hepsie to this, 'how do you think I could face your father in the next world if harm came to you through me? If we can but think of a scheme to trick these watchdogs your cousin's set on you, you'll go without any more argument, my girl.'

And in the end it was Hepsie who found the way out. With much misgiving, because the escape route was not without its dangers, she suggested that the girl should climb down the old quarry face that formed part of the estate boundary. Much of the stone that had gone into the original house had been taken from the quarry, but it had not been worked for years. It was considerably overgrown with shrubs and young trees, which would afford handholds in the descent, and surely, because of its precipitous nature, it would not be guarded. No one would dream that a girl would adventure so perilous a route.

'But there *is* a track, that I *do* know,' insisted Hepsie, 'for many's the time I've taken your father a picnic dinner to the old tree at the quarry edge when he was a boy. Hours he would spend there, watching the birds. And you can't mistake the tree because it has two trunks.'

Chantal knew it at once, and was sure that she could find her way there by moonlight. She was a good deal less confident about the rest of the adventure. She was not over fond of heights, and what was perfectly possible for an active lad in broad daylight might not be so easy for a girl and in the dark. But it was the only way that they could think of, and better to fall and break her neck than to lie helpless here like some trapped bird awaiting the approach of the fowler.

'Then if you're going, best go at once,' said Hepsie firmly. 'Tonight. The moon will serve well enough. I don't know when his lordship's expected back, but the nearer the time the closer you'll be watched.'

And so it was agreed. They spent the afternoon in quietness, each knowing that they were unlikely to meet again in this world, each trying to hide the knowledge from the other. Only at the end, her few preparations made, Hepsie's kiss still warm on her cheek, did Chantal falter for a moment when the old woman whispered, 'I'll tell him that you faced trouble bravely, as he would have wished.'

Then the door closed softly behind her and she was slipping through the familiar corridors, blessedly dark at the moment, to a little-used door that opened on to the terraces at the side of the house.

The first part of her journey was

uneventful. The grounds were as familiar as her own rooms, and she slipped softly from tree to tree, only her face and hands briefly visible in the moonlight. Hepsie had suggested that she wear a black dress, and together they had cut off the skirt almost up to the knee so that it should not hamper her. 'Though what they'll think of you at the. Pelican I shame to think,' Hepsie had grunted crossly. 'You look like some gypsy hoyden.' And Chantal had retorted cheerfully that as long as the gold was good, mine host at the Pelican would hire his vehicles to an escaping criminal still dangling his fetters.

'Well, it's to be hoped he doesn't think you stole the money and send for a constable,' sighed Hepsie, testing the knots that secured the money bag about the girl's waist to leave her hands free.

The sovereigns jingled softly in their leather pouch, but now there was only herself to hear the tiny noise. So far the plan had worked well. But here was the twin-trunked tree that marked the beginning of the track, and now she must face a new danger.

The moon, which had so far befriended her, was of no help here. Its light did not penetrate into the abyss. Perhaps that was as well, she decided, trying to ignore the nervous dread that possessed her.

'Papa would be ashamed of you,' she told herself severely. And was startled at the sound of her own voice, loud in the quiet night.

It frightened her into beginning the descent. Suppose any one had been near enough to hear her! It would be dreadful to be recaptured having got so far. And after all it wasn't so bad as she had expected. There was no hope of picking out the track in the darkness. All she could do was feel her way forward and downward, clinging to trees and rocks for security. Once or twice she had to make a traverse to avoid ledges that dropped sheer – it might be two feet, it might be twenty. In the darkness she had no means of knowing. Her progress was erratic and undignified. She slid and crawled rather than walked, and once or twice some seemingly secure handhold gave way under her weight and she rolled over and over, clutching fiercely at bushes and brambles, anything that would check her headlong passage. But already quite a comforting proportion of the cliff loomed above her. She took heart and pressed on.

She was, in fact, quite close to the bottom when disaster overtook her. She had reached a stretch of scree. The slope was steep and the stuff moved under her feet, but there seemed to be no way round it. Anxiously she embarked on the treacherous crossing, starting a small avalanche of stones at each hesitant step. There was nothing here to cling to, and now there were bigger stones on the move. She lowered herself to the ground and tried sliding. It felt safer, but it moved more stones. The noise must be audible for some distance. Desperately she struggled on, praying that she had not yet been missed, for if there were search parties out looking for her the racket she was making would bring them like hounds to a view. Down, down, until a pursuing boulder, disturbed in her struggles, struck her a glancing blow on the side of her head and dropped her neatly into the pool of water that lay at the quarry foot.

Two

Chantal opened her eyes to clear sunshine, and promptly closed them again as pain stabbed through her temples. The pain subsided a little and she put up a tentative hand to her head. It felt bruised and tender. She lay trying to recall what had happened to her, but she could remember nothing after her struggles with the scree. With a shiver of fear she wondered if her cousin's servants had found her; if she was even now being carried back to captivity. For she was certainly travelling in some kind of vehicle, though by the bumping, lurching nature of its progress she doubted if it was one of the carriages from the Court.

She put up a hand to shield her eyes from the light, which came through a tiny window no more than a foot square, and peeped cautiously through her fingers. She was lying in a narrow bed, rather like the sleeping berths in the cabin of her father's yacht, and the further she looked the more marked grew the resemblance to a ship. The vehicle was a little house on wheels, its furniture and fittings of the simplest, and most of them seemed to be screwed to the floor, which was just as well in view of the roughness of transit. The lamp that was affixed to the wall over the bed was swinging wildly and a clatter of crockery sounded a protest from a cupboard. There was a mirror fitted over a chest which had a padded top and obviously served also as a stool, and a curtain over one corner which might conceal clothing. A piece of heavy canvas covered a doorway at one end which presumably led to the box or the driving seat or whatever one called it in this type of vehicle. Chantal thought it must be some type of gypsy van, and for one fantastic moment wondered if she had actually been carried off by a band of these strange folk for the sake of the gold she carried. But that *must* be nonsense. If they had found her unconscious they had only to take the money and leave her to her fate. It seemed more probable that some kind Samaritan had stumbled upon her and was, perhaps, taking her to some place where her hurts could be attended to. Now that she came to consider the matter, she discovered quite a number of hurts. Her arms were covered with grazes and bruises, though only the bump on her head caused her any serious discomfort, and every muscle shrieked a protest at the unusual exertions to which it had been subjected.

It was at this stage of her investigations that she discovered that she was naked. A blanket had been tucked round her, but some one had removed every stitch of her clothing. Thoroughly startled and not a little frightened, she tried to sit up. The effort made her feel giddy and sick. It also produced an upheaval from under the bed on which she was lying. A dog – she could only suppose it was a dog, though never before had she seen such an impressive specimen – had evidently been sharing her slumbers, and now emerged with some difficulty from the confined space to rear up and plant heavy forepaws on her body. A massive head, with deeply wrinkled brow and long drooping ears was inclined towards her as the creature snuffed at her face. But its disposition seemed to be amiable, and presently, as though satisfied that she meant no harm, it settled itself beside the bed, its great jowl resting on the quilt that had been thrown over her, its mournful eyes fixed on her face. She put out a timid hand to smooth the silken head. The caress was accepted with enthusiasm, the head nudged forward for further favours. Plainly it would be quite safe to venture out of bed and explore further. But there was no sign of her clothes, and to be parading about exiguously attired in a blanket was not quite to her taste.

At this point the van lurched to a halt. The dog got up, nosed aside the canvas door-cover, and disappeared round it. She heard a man's voice say, 'And has your wretched bit of flotsam recovered its senses yet, Jester?'

It was an attractive voice, a cultured voice, and certainly not what one would expect of a gypsy or pedlar. Flotsam was floating wreckage. If she had been pulled out of some stream or lake, that would account for her present attire – or lack of it – though it did nothing to diminish the consequent embarrassment. She pulled the quilt up to her throat and waited for the owner of the voice to appear. Instead she heard sounds indicating that he was attending to his horse. She began to feel slightly indignant. Surely a girl was more important than a horse, especially a girl who had been saved from a watery death and who must pose something of a mystery. She waited in a growing impatience which helped her to forget her shameful nakedness.

The wait was a very long one. There was no sound now from outside. Had he gone to summon a physician? Or, terrifying thought, a constable? The pain in her head was much better, but she was beginning to feel faint with hunger. She lay watching the shadows lengthen until she could endure no longer. If her rescuer would not come to her, she would go to him. She folded the blanket in half and draped it over her shoulders, toga fashion. A search for some belt or tie to hold it in position produced only a long leather leash. It would have to serve. She wound it two or three times round her slender middle and knotted it as firmly as the leather would permit. Then, with fast beating heart, she pushed aside the canvas cover and looked out.

There were two horses grazing in the forest glade in which the caravan had come to rest. One was a sturdy dapple grey, some sixteen hands she estimated, young but of heavy build. The other was the finest thoroughbred mare she had ever set eyes on. Of human presence there was no sign. She lowered herself painfully to the ground and walked round the van, one hand resting on its gaily painted panels for support, to stop short, aware of rising anger, at the scene that met her eyes.

An easel had been erected at the other end of the glade, and standing in front of it was a tall man, dressed in rough fustian breeches and a shepherd's smock, liberally splashed with paint. So absorbed was he in his painting that he did not even notice her approach until the dog got up and came to greet her. Then he *did* look up briefly, gave her one quick, frowning glance and said curtly, 'You'll have to wait. The light's going.'

Whatever Chantal had expected, it was not this. But strangely enough the abrupt dismissal had an unexpectedly reassuring effect. In the few minutes that elapsed before he threw down the brush with a grunt of annoyance, she had time to notice several things. First, that the view he was painting was entirely strange to her, and since she knew the countryside in the neighbourhood of Delaney Court pretty well, she could only assume that they had travelled some distance. A comforting thought. From the outset she had been anxious about the journey to London, fearful that she might not outstrip a really determined pursuit.

But no one was likely to look for her here.

Secondly she was thankful to discover her clothes, spread on some bushes in a patch of sunlight, and to find that her undergarments, at least, were very nearly dry. She busied herself with turning the dress so that the damp breadths were exposed to the sun, though by the look of it she was unlikely to be able to wear it again.

Presently the artist, having put his gear in some sort of order, came towards her, according her a cool assessing gaze. In a ballroom she would have given him a smart set-down for that, she though inconsequently, and smiled a little at the recollection of her incongruous attire. Quite what she expected him to say, she did not know. Probably some polite enquiry as to her health, and in what way he could be of service to her. After that it might be difficult. She had no thought of taking a stranger into her confidence, even if he *had* pulled her out of the water. So it was disconcerting, to say the least, when the gentleman said indifferently, 'Your duds are about dry. You can get dressed in the van and then be on your way.'

Any lingering doubt that her rescuer might be inclined to take advantage of her defenceless position was promptly banished. Indeed it seemed slightly surprising that he had put himself to the trouble of pulling her out of the water, and it was this thought that found expression.

There was a flicker of surprise in the gentleman's blue gaze, a faint lifting of the dark brows. Even in indignation, Chantal's voice was low and musical. It was his turn to be surprised at a purity of accent that matched his own in one whom he had taken to be some wandering gypsy lass. Curiosity stirred within him, but he refused to admit it.

'You may thank Jester for that,' he said lightly, dropping one hand on the head of the animal that stood beside him. 'It was she who heard your descent into the pool and was insistent that you be rescued.'

Perhaps it was the very unconcern in the gentleman's voice that drove Chantal to some attempt at justification. 'I managed the quarry face pretty well,' she said, a hint of defiance in the tilt of her chin. 'It was the scree that proved my undoing.'

'As many a rash mountaineer has found before you,' he agreed. And then, his interest now fully engaged, for if she had indeed come down that quarry face there must have been an urgent reason, 'Had it not been for Jester you might have drowned. Your escapade was both ill-judged and reckless.'

Such scathing criticism from one who knew nothing of the circumstances stung her to prompt retort, as he had expected.

'It was *not* an escapade,' she told him hotly. 'I was running away from the most odious persecution. Nothing less would have driven me to the attempt, for I hate heights.'

From in-bred courtesy he hid his amusement. These schoolgirls! His cousins were just the same. He wondered what small domestic injustice had driven this one to such lengths, for say what you would, it had taken courage to attempt that descent. He supposed he would have to spend a little more time and trouble on the chit than he had at first intended.

'Then I owe you an apology,' he said politely. 'Pray tell me how I can be of service.'

'Well you could give me something to eat,' she suggested practically. 'I'm starving of hunger.'

The remark confirmed his estimate of her youthful status. He relaxed. 'Into the van with you, then, and get dressed, and I'll see what I can do.'

She gathered up her possessions and obeyed him promptly, but nothing would make her gown fit to wear. The skirt was in tatters. Her shoes were missing and her stockings were in holes. When she emerged from the van she looked much the same as when she had gone in, bare-legged and blanket-clad.

He frowned at this but made no comment, proffering a plate of bread and cold meat and a glass of milk. He had made no preparations to eat with her. She hoped she was not robbing him of his own lunch but she was too hungry to waste overmuch sympathy on him. He watched her for a moment, deciding that she had not overstated the case when she had claimed to be starving, and then turned away, leaving her to eat in peace while he packed away his painting materials and began preparations for moving on. Presently he came back, her money bag in one hand, a couple of apples in the other.

'Better check your money,' he suggested stiffly. 'And as soon as you are done I would like the blanket. I want to reach Claverton before dusk. If you follow that track' – he pointed it out – 'you will come to

Trowbridge where you can either find accommodation or book yourself a seat on the stage.'

She looked up at him in startled dismay. Surely he did not mean to abandon her here? She said desperately, 'Oh – please – you said you would help me. I can't walk into a village without any shoes and my gown in ribbons. Indeed I don't mean to be a trouble to you, but you must see that I can't.'

'And what, exactly, do you expect me to do about it?' he enquired grimly.

'Well I thought perhaps you could buy me a dress – any kind of dress, just so that I look respectable – and some shoes and a shawl. I've got plenty of money,' she placated eagerly.

He could scarcely have looked more horrified if she had asked him to buy her a shift, but she was too concerned to see anything humorous in his expression of dismay. He looked down at the slender bare feet that peeped beneath the blanket. It was no good telling himself that her troubles were of her own making. He could not bring himself to drive off and leave her in such a case. But neither did he intend to venture into some haunt of female fashion.

'Not for all the money in your purse,' he told her firmly. 'There's only one thing to be done. You'll have to come home with me. Then one of the maids can go shopping for you. And the next time you insist on rescuing a half-drowned kitten,' he told the dog, 'I shall throw it back again.'

It seemed to Chantal that a meek, appreciative silence was her best rôle. She applied herself to an apple.

Her reluctant host said suddenly, 'What's more I'm not taking you up in front in *that* rig. It only needs a feather in your hair and you'll pass for Pocahontas herself. You'll have to travel in the van and you'll be devilish uncomfortable. But wait a minute! I believe–' He sprang up into the van and came back in a moment carrying a wrapper of crimson silk which he thrust into her arms. 'There! Put that on. No one will see your feet, and at a distance it will pass for a dress.'

Chantal accepted the proffered garment before he could change his mind. She was mildly intrigued by the wrapper, a very feminine garment indeed, which looked exactly what it was – a luxurious dressing gown. But if her benefactor thought it would pass as a dress, she didn't mean to disillusion him. She studied her reflection in the inadequate looking glass and tied the girdle about her waist, spirits rising insensibly at the caress of the silken stuff against her skin, then folded the blanket neatly and laid it on the bed, dropping the money bag on top of it. That done she pushed aside the canvas screen.

The driving seat did not offer much greater comfort than the inside of the van. It was just a plain wooden bench. But at least one could see the country-side, and every mile towards Claverton was taking her further from the Court. The start was slightly delayed by the dog's desire to share the narrow bench, but a stern word from her master sent her to sit on the floor between them, where she heaved a reproachful sigh and laid a heavy head on Chantal's lap.

Until they left the woods behind conversation was impossible, but after a few minutes they emerged into a narrow lane where the surface was reasonably smooth. Of an open and friendly disposition herself, it did not occur to Chantal that her companion might prefer to travel in silence. The journey must take some three or four hours and there was nothing to see but flowering hedgerows and an occasional farmhouse. She sought about her for some impersonal topic and found it in the heavy head that rested on her knee.

'What made you call her Jester? She looks so mournful that it is the last thing I would have thought of.'

He considered the trivial question gravely. Then said, 'Well – she is parti-coloured – black and tan for a jester's red and yellow – and as for her sorrowful looks, do not all jesters traditionally suffer from broken hearts?'

She fondled the silken ears. 'You're a beautiful dog, aren't you, my rescuer,' she crooned, 'despite your jaundiced expression.'

'Not dog. Hound,' corrected the animal's owner. 'Have you never seen a bloodhound before?'

She shook her head. 'Foxhounds and otterhounds, but never a bloodhound. I've heard of them, though. I thought they were very fierce and savage. Are they not used to track down fugitives? Escaped slaves in the Cotton States, and dangerous criminals?'

Her random choice of topic had been an excellent one. She was promptly enlightened as to the temperament, habits and usefulness of the bloodhound and the methods used in training, a lecture which only terminated when the specimen beside her raised that intelligent head and yawned her boredom, which had the beneficial effect of making her master laugh.

The transformation was surprising. Chantal had thought him quite a good looking sort of man in his loose-limbed untidy way, but she did not care for his expression. She thought him supercilious. Perhaps it was the effect of the narrow black moustache and the neatly pointed beard that he wore. They gave him the air of some lofty grandee in a Velasquez portrait. Chantal, who preferred her men clean-shaven, like Papa, privately described it as 'sneery'. But when the blue eyes lit to laughter and the firm lips parted to show excellent white teeth, he looked years younger and much more approachable.

She was emboldened to ask one or two questions about his home. Would there be shops close at hand, where she could purchase what was needed to supplement her scanty wardrobe? Was there a regular mail coach service or would it be better to hire a post chaise? And would she need to stay overnight at an inn or would they reach Claverton in time for her to continue her journey?

'Because, you see, until I reach London I must make do with the money that I have with me, and I am not very sure about the cost of the journey,' she ended diffidently.

The talk about Jester had broken the ice. Her questions stirred his curiosity. He answered them to the best of his ability, explaining that it was his brother's house. His knowledge of the shopping facilities was naturally sketchy, but the housekeeper would know. 'And you couldn't reach London without spending at least one night on the road,' he ended, 'so you might just as well stay in Claverton. I would offer you over-night hospitality – my brother's – but it would not do for you to be staying in a bachelor household.'

His expression of grave concern was the last straw. To think that he should be worrying over her reputation after all that she had gone through during the past twenty four hours induced a paroxysm of irresistible mirth. She bowed her head over Jester's and gave way to helpless, healing laughter. His puzzled face when at last she stopped to draw breath nearly set her off again but she managed to control herself sufficiently to explain her sentiments.

'Naturally I realise that after spending the night in your van I haven't a shred of reputation left to me,' she ended calmly, 'but as an alternative to marrying my cousin it seems a light penalty. Indeed, even drowning would have been preferable.'

'You certainly spoke of persecution,' he said slowly, 'but I had not realised that you were bent on avoiding a distasteful marriage. It is quite your own affair, of course, but if you have cut yourself adrift from your home, are you assured of some shelter and some means of support? You speak of going to London. Have you friends there?'

For a moment she hesitated. He *seemed* quite trustworthy, but her confidence in her own judgement had been rudely shaken of late. On the other hand he had treated her kindly, if brusquely, and she still needed his help in arranging her journey. It might be interesting, too, to see how a stranger reacted to her story.

'I plan to go to my father's attorney,' she explained. 'He is one of my guardians and has charge of all my financial affairs. Once I can place myself under his protection I shall be quite safe. But my situation is complicated, partly by my own past follies.'

She proceeded to outline the circumstances

leading to her present difficulties. He listened attentively and, she thought, with some sympathy. Coming to an end she said, 'It seems odd to be telling all this to a stranger. We do not even know each other's names. Mine is Delaney. Chantal Delaney. My father was the Earl of Hilsborough.'

She sensed immediately the withdrawal of his sympathy. He said grimly, 'I have heard of you, ma'am. Or perhaps I should rather say that I have heard tales of some of your – exploits. One can well see how they lent substance to your cousin's fabrications. You have been taught a sharp lesson – not undeserved – and will be more circumspect in future.'

He did not volunteer his own name, nor evince any further interest in her plans or her difficulties. Chantal bowed her head over the hound. She had undergone a considerable ordeal. The future was still uncertain, promising a difficult and lonely road. Moreover her head was beginning to ache again. But not for worlds would she let him see the tears that his harsh words had brought to her eyes. She made pretence of being fully occupied with the hound.

His hearing was sharp. She did not sob or gulp, but he caught the quivering indrawn breath and a swift glance showed bright drops sliding down Jester's neck.

He said impatiently, 'You think me unfair. Well – I have good cause to detest your kind. Frivolous empty-headed society maidens with no other thought than to entrap or befool the men their pretty faces have dazzled. One of your stamp was responsible for wrecking my brother's life. I have not forgotten – or forgiven.'

It was some time before she could trust her voice to answer and she still kept her head bowed. She said quietly, 'It would certainly seem unfair to condemn an entire social group for the failings of one or two of its members. I am not defending myself. I am well aware that I behaved foolishly. But I know many girls of my class who are loving and loyal wives and devoted mothers. They are not all frivolous and selfish.'

Since he knew very well that she was right there could be no answering her calm good sense. He said savagely, 'Very well, then. I listened to *your* story. Now hear mine. My brother was just twenty two, a fine athlete, a first-rate shot – in fact a capital good fellow when he lost his heart to a silly simpering miss with a passion for anything that wore regimentals. Oliver was no soldier. His days were fully occupied in managing my father's estates, to which, incidentally, he is heir. Doubtless his prospective rank and wealth outweighed his shortcomings in the way of military glamour and his inamorata consented to a betrothal. This was in '15. When Boney got loose and the whole thing looked like being to do over again, nothing would serve for Isabella but that Oliver should join the army. This time he agreed with her. The need was urgent. He rode well – was a good shot – and so forth. But the idea would never have entered his head if she had not put it there, and all for vanity and to gratify her foolish whim. To be brief, in his first engagement – and that no glorious battle but a mere clash between patrol and outpost – he was struck in the face by a spent bullet. As a result he lost the sight of one eye. Worse than that, in falling from his horse he injured his spine, so that he is now a helpless husk of a man. How do you think Isabella's military fervour stood the test? Naturally Oliver insisted on releasing her from their engagement. Such a marriage could be no marriage. I do not blame her for feeling herself inadequate to that sacrifice. But within the month she announced her engagement to one of the

'Gentlemen's Sons' – a pink-cheeked halfling who never even got as far as Brussels, but who looked extremely picturesque in his scarlet and gold. Nor was that the end of the mischief. My father, upon seeing the condition of the son in whom he had taken such loving pride, succumbed to an apoplectic seizure and lay helpless for months, though he is now somewhat restored. But the sight of Oliver's affliction worked so powerfully upon him that the physicians insisted that they be kept apart. So my father spends most of his time in Town while Oliver divides his between our Midlands home and Claverton – it was hoped at one time that a course of the waters at Bath might prove beneficial – and they rarely meet. Poor Mama is torn between the two of them. When she is with Papa she worries about Oliver – and vice versa. Do you wonder that I have little time for shallow-pated débutantes?'

Chantal considered her reply with care. Her tender heart was wrung with pity for a young man struck down in the flower of his youth, but it was obvious that expressions of sympathy would be ill-received. She said quietly, 'How old were you at the time of the tragedy?'

His reply was almost sullen. 'Fourteen. And what has that to do with anything?'

'Only that it seems unlikely that either party confided in you at the time,' she pointed out. 'So you are basing your judgement on hearsay evidence.' And just the right age for hero worship of a splendid elder brother and – possibly – jealousy of that brother's preoccupation with a mere female. Though of that one could not be sure.

He did not deign to answer this very patent truth but turned the attack neatly by saying, 'At least I need not lay myself open to that charge where you are concerned, since you may speak in your own defence. I will not ask if you were the toast of the town, your admirers legion, your name on everyone's lips. So much is common knowledge and modesty might compel you to dissimulate. Tell me instead, is it true that you appeared at your début in cloth of gold and emeralds? That during some ball or other you were seen to smoke a cigar in the conservatory? Do you not always ride astride in male attire? and were you not the cause of two duels?'

Her head titled defiantly. 'The first three, yes. And many more foolish pranks, the evidence of ignorance and youthful high spirits, for which, as you pronounced, I am being well punished. Though as regards the riding I had my Papa's approval. He said side saddles were an invention of the devil – unkind to the horse and dangerous for the rider. The duels are a different matter. Are you not old enough to know that if gentlemen in their cups choose to quarrel, they will find some cause, whether it be a notorious débutante or the suspect running of a fancied horse. I knew nothing of either meeting until it was over, and could not have stopped them if I had, since I was barely acquainted with the protagonists. Any more than your brother's betrothed could have deflected the bullet that struck him down. You may say that she was foolish – shallow – fickle – but you cannot in honesty blame her for the other misfortunes that befell your family. Your brother might have suffered just such an incapacitating fall in the hunting field. Neither have you the right to condemn me as equally beneath your contempt, just because you have heard gossip about a headstrong girl's follies. Did you never kick over the traces yourself when you were young, or were you always a model of decorum?'

'At the moment it is not *my* conduct that is in question,' he reminded her. 'But I confess myself at fault in taking you to task for yours. I beg your pardon. On this head we are unlikely to agree. Perhaps you will just accept the fact that, since I dislike women, more especially the useless ornaments of society, I am not inclined to put myself to any particular trouble on your behalf. Once you are adequately equipped for your journey, my part is played.'

'In that case I will thank you now for your share in my rescue,' she said equably, and then recalled that his services had included the removal of her soaked clothing. Her lips twitched slightly. 'In face of your expressed views it must have been a most distasteful task,' she said thoughtfully. 'I am most truly grateful.'

He did not pretend to misunderstand her. One did not expect proper modesty from such as Lady Chantal, but this impudence passed all bounds and merited swift punishment.

'Extremely distasteful,' he told her languidly. 'But I really couldn't permit you to soak my bedding. It was only that thought that steeled me to the task of stripping you.'

It should have reduced her to blushful

silence. Instead he distinctly heard a smothered chuckle. She said gently, 'Now you may rest content. You have certainly paid off any score you had against me. How thankful I shall be to exchange your protection for dear Mr. Dickensen's.'

The placid dapple grey checked abruptly. Chantal glanced up in surprise. Her companion was frowning grimly and staring ahead of him, apparently unaware that he had halted the beast.

'*Who* did you say?' he demanded sharply.

'Mr. Dickensen. My father's attorney.'

'Mr. *Roger* Dickensen? Of Albemarle Street?'

'Yes. That is he. Do you know him?'

He did not answer immediately. Instead he turned towards her and somewhat unexpectedly put one warm strong hand over hers. He said quietly, 'It distresses me to have to give you bad news, but it is better that you should hear it now before you embark on a fruitless journey to London. Your old friend is no more. He was the victim of a brutal attack in the street as he made his way home from his club, and he died of his injuries.'

Three

'Under the circumstances, my good girl, your scruples are perfectly ridiculous.' The words had a familiar ring in Chantal's ears. Cousin Giffard, she recalled, had voiced similar sentiments. Could it be only twenty four hours ago? But the speaker and the circumstances to which he referred were vastly different. Nor was there any sneer in the voice, though a good deal of impatience with feminine foibles.

And to speak truth she would dearly love to yield to his guidance. The news of Mr. Dickensen's death had been a severe shock. She had never known the lawyer intimately for he was older even than her father and was, moreover, a bachelor, so that during her schooldays she had not come much in his way. But when they *had* chanced to meet his manner towards her had always been kind and gentle and he had been *there*, in the background of her life, a man of wisdom and experience to whom one could turn with confidence in time of need. Now he was gone. And at the edge of her mind was the first faint suspicion that his death might in some way be connected with his responsibility for the affairs of one Chantal Delaney. Her cousin had shown himself quite unscrupulous. He had said something about fobbing off enquiries from her friends. Mr. Dickensen was not one to be easily fobbed off where his duty was concerned. How if stronger measures had been used?

She shook herself impatiently. This was – must be – the merest hysteria. She might have endured a good deal, including a blow on the head, but that was no reason for yielding to morbid fancies, she told herself firmly. The unpleasant idea refused to be banished entirely. It strengthened her desire to fall in with her rescuer's plans, while at the same time she was more than ever determined that *he* should not be involved in her unsavoury affairs.

'It was you who said that once I was suitably equipped for my journey your responsibility would be at an end,' she reminded him. 'Mr. Dickensen's death does not alter that.'

'Of course it does,' he said brusquely. 'I made that statement in the belief that you were seeking shelter with a responsible guardian. Where, now, will you turn?'

'I shall go to the Shapleys. My father left me with Mrs. Shapley when he went to Afghanistan. Rose Shapley and I were school friends and we made our come-out together. It was only after Papa's death that I went home to the Court. There was no reason why my bereavement should be permitted to spoil Rose's chances. But my year of mourning is past, so I daresay Mrs. Shapley will be quite willing to take me in.'

'Is there a Mr. Shapley?'

She shook her head. 'He died when Rose was quite a small girl. She scarcely remembers him.'

'Then I do not think it a suitable home for you under present circumstances. If there is indeed a plot to trap you into marriage with your cousin, then some effort will be made to persuade or even force you to return to your home. The death of your other guardian leaves you in a very vulnerable position, since you are not, I assume, of age.'

Her anxious air, the lower lip caught between her teeth, admitted the force of his argument.

'Very well, then. How do you think this

Mrs. Shapley of yours would stand up to pressure from your relatives? Perfectly reasonable, legitimate pressure, remember, probably backed up by a hint that you are too high-strung and sensitive to be the best judge of what is good for you.'

The big grey eyes, enormous and shadowed in her strained face, gave him his answer. He nodded. 'In such a case you need a man's firmness to support you.'

'Well I shall have to make do as well as I may without it,' she retorted tartly. And then, a hint of mischief lightening her expression, 'But pray advise me, sir. If *you* were the head of the Shapley household, how would *you* set about so awkward a business?'

If she had thought to take him at fault she was disappointed.

'Keep you close hid, for a start, and deny all knowledge of you. To all intents and purposes you would be a prisoner, but it's the only safe way. What's more I'd shift your quarters every month or so, so that no rumour of a strange female seen strolling in the gardens or glimpsed through a window could bring suspicion upon me. You would have to co-operate, of course. Such close confinement might not suit the wilful Lady Chantal.'

She studied him, intrigued. Outlining his plan, he sounded quite different, crisp and competent, the man of action rather than the idle dilettante of her first impression.

She said slowly, 'You make very free with *my* name, sir, but have not seen fit to entrust me with yours. Perhaps I trespass. Perhaps you are some great gentleman – travelling incognito. I should beg pardon for my presumption – and congratulate you on the disguise. It is excellent.'

He eyed her levelly. 'Throwing your tongue, aren't you, my girl? Don't forget that you still depend on my help. That's unless you choose to walk into the village barefoot and clad in that rather exotic dressing gown. I can think of nothing better calculated to draw attention to your presence here, but if that is your wish–' He shrugged.

Chantal flushed. Her words had been scarce uttered before they were regretted for the jibe was undeserved. If he had not displayed any marked courtesy towards her, he had certainly not behaved ungentleman-like. She could not imagine what had made her rip up at him like that and words of apology were already clotting her tongue.

Again he surprised her. 'And that was as near to blackmail as makes no difference,' he said ruefully. 'You seem to have a deplorable effect on my moral principles. Please believe that I did not intend to implement my threat.'

That made it easy. 'If you, in turn, will forgive my shocking rudeness,' she said impulsively, and turned to smile at him, a little shyly. 'It was horrid of me, for you had done nothing to deserve it. Indeed I have felt very comfortable while I have been in your care.'

He smiled at her delightfully. Whether because of her frank apology or because she had given him just the opening that he desired, she was not afterwards quite sure.

'Then you are not really so anxious to be quit of me, are you?' he suggested gently. And before she could protest went on, 'I'll tell you what. We'll tell the whole tangled tale to Oliver and let him decide what's best to be done. You don't know him yet, but I can honestly say that if I was in any kind of a fix there's no one I'd rather go to.' He seemed to consider this pronouncement for a moment, then went on, 'He's perceptive. Shut away from the world as he is, you might not expect it. But it seems as if all his energies have been channelled into his mind. Do I sound maudlin? You'll understand when you meet him. As for my name, I'm Dominic Merriden. Oliver always calls me Nick, but despite my lack of manners I am not, I trust, wholly devoted to evil. Indeed I always understood that the devil was a rather polished creature, so perhaps my boorishness is my best advocate.'

The name had a familiar ring though she could not immediately place it. That was hardly surprising. If Mr. Merriden had been fourteen in the year of the great battle he must be past thirty now, and was hardly likely to frequent the circles which Chantal had known during her one brief season. But the warmth of his smile, the frank friendliness of his new approach, combined with her own instinctive desires to win her agreement.

'Very well, sir,' she conceded. 'It shall be as you wish.'

He urged the horse to renewed activity. 'I think you are wise,' he said. 'I will send a servant to engage rooms for you at the White Hart, and one of the maids shall go with you to appease the proprieties. Mrs. Baxter – Oliver's housekeeper – will know which wench to choose. One that can be trusted not to tattle.'

Chantal protested that she was giving a great deal of trouble. Surely it was unnecessary to take an abigail with her for so short a stay as she would be making.

'We wish your appearance to be as unremarkable as possible,' he reminded her. 'Even when you are decently gowned and have purchased such articles as you require for your toilet, you still have no luggage. I could lend you a valise, but trunks and band boxes such as women use are beyond my touch, while to have everything brand new would in itself be suspicious. So you have a maid, and you can scold her if you so wish for her carelessness in losing your baggage. That will serve to explain your forlorn state to the landlord's satisfaction.'

'Your talent for intrigue is admirable, sir,' she told him politely. 'Does it also furnish me with a credible reason for being in the neighbourhood?'

'Not at the moment,' he admitted. 'Perhaps Oliver will think of one for us. And since you seem unduly concerned over the trouble you are making, let me assure you that where Oliver is concerned your arrival is an unmitigated boon.'

She raised her brows a little at that, and

chose her words carefully. 'Your brother does not, then, share your aversion to my sex?'

'Oliver just likes people, regardless of sex, as also of wealth or social consequence. A new acquaintance, especially one with a problem, is to him like some rare volume to an ardent bibliophile. As you can imagine, his activities are sadly limited, and it is an object with all of us to keep him as well entertained as possible. In distracting him from the tedium of his days you will be performing an act of pure charity.'

She could not help laughing a little. She understood his motive in telling her what must serve to ease the burden of obligation and liked him the better for this thoughtfulness, but need he have been quite so blunt? To be likened to a book provided for the distraction of an invalid was not calculated to set any woman up in her own esteem! Prolonged association with Mr. Merriden seemed likely to prove a salutory experience for one who had been more accustomed to hear subtle compliment and soothing flattery than straightforward truth!

From speaking of his brother he passed easily to talk of the Claverton house whither they were bound. She learned that both boys had spent a good deal of time there as children and were still fond of the place. A simple question set him off again on the breeding and personality of the thoroughbred mare trotting so obediently behind them, and since this was a subject with a strong appeal for Chantal the talk ran easily and they were quite in charity with each other when the caravan finally creaked through the gates of Old Hall. Not the main gates, of course. Such a vehicle – and such a passenger – passed modestly through a farm gate that was more generally used for the delivery of straw and fodder to the stables.

Two grooms came running out to take the horses. Mr. Merriden gave brief instructions as to their disposal and ended by saying to the older of the two, 'And then come up to the house. I'll want a note taken down to the White Hart.'

He then turned to his passenger. 'Better let me lift you down,' he told her carelessly. 'These cobble stones are hard on the feet.' And as she gave herself into his hold, carried her easily through the arched stable entrance and set her down on the soft turf that stretched smoothly towards the house.

Now that they had reached civilisation – and civilisation expressed in all the gracious dignity of an old and well tended house – Chantal was very conscious of the deficiencies in her raiment. She was thankful that her host led her to a small side door which gave access first to a conservatory and then to a morning room, where her sartorial shame could be decently hidden from curious eyes.

'Now for Oliver,' he said cheerfully. 'He usually sits in the library at this hour of day.'

She would have known them for brothers, Chantal decided. Not so much from physical resemblance, for though their features were cast in a similar mould, Oliver's colouring was more subdued – his eyes grey where his brother's were blue, his hair a lightish brown and his hands and complexion inevitably betraying the mark of his indoor existence. But their voices held the same intonations, their mannerisms were similar and their thoughts chimed so easily together that much of their talk was conducted in half sentences.

Her first impression was that there was nothing in the older man's appearance to shock or disgust even a sensitive person.

Apart from the neat black patch over one eye and the fact that he was seated in a light wheeled chair with a rug cast over his knees, there was no suggestion of invalidism. His coat was a good deal better cut than the one for which Dominic had exchanged his paint-smeared smock, his hair and his neck-cloth arranged with exquisite neatness. So much she had time to assimilate as she heard Dominic say, 'You will permit me to present my brother Oliver, Lady Chantal? Oliver I have brought you a fugitive in need of wise guidance. Lady Chantal Delaney.'

She curtsied and held out her hand. It was taken in a firm clasp, a look of half-amused concern was bent upon her as the gentleman said quietly, 'How seriously am I to take that, Lady Chantal? With my brother one can never be sure. He delights in making game of me. Then when he has me fooled to the top of his bent, he will admit it was all a hoax. I know of you by repute, of course, and I was a little acquainted with your father. I cannot imagine that his daughter would stand in any need of advice from me, honoured and delighted as I would be to serve you.'

'It is true enough, sir,' she told him. 'Your

brother has been so good as to promise his help in my immediate necessities' – she indicated her dress – 'but there are other problems. Mr. Merriden was insistent that you were the very man to advise me, and though I am naturally loath to burden a stranger with my troubles I am bound to confess that I myself cannot hit upon a solution. I would be grateful indeed for any advice that you could offer.'

He studied her gravely, a slight frown furrowing the white brow, as he begged her to be seated and asked if she would partake of any refreshment.

'Your brother was so kind as to feed me,' she explained, 'but I would be glad if he could make the necessary arrangements to buy me some shoes and a gown as soon as may be. It is odd how defenceless one feels when one is improperly dressed.'

He smiled a little for that and looked enquiringly at Dominic. The latter had risen and moved towards the window. 'Someone coming,' he said over his shoulder. 'A coach and four, too, with outriders and at least one other vehicle by the sound of it. Now who is coming a-visiting in such state? Can Lady Chantal's family have picked up her trail already, and arrived with reinforcements to bear her off in our teeth?'

The girl whitened a little at the mischievous suggestion. Oliver said quite firmly, 'That's enough of your nonsense, Nick. You know very well that it isn't so – and even if it was, we are quite capable of holding our own.'

'Only she isn't our own,' retorted Dominic, turning with interest towards the library door where footsteps could be heard approaching. The door was thrown open and a lady came hurrying in.

Chantal, only too well aware of the appearance she presented, shrank back in the shelter of her winged chair. Dominic started forward in welcome and Oliver exclaimed delightedly, 'Mama! How perfectly splendid! We didn't expect you till next month.'

'Is all well at home? Papa in pretty good shape?' enquired Dominic.

His mother hugged as much of him as she could manage in one arm since Oliver was still clasping her other hand. 'In very good shape,' she assured him briskly. 'But I had to do something quickly to ward off one of his worst attacks.' She smiled mischievously. 'Your Aunt Arabella wrote that she planned to spend a month with us this year! You can imagine Papa's sentiments! Last year was nearly the end of him, he vowed, and she only stayed a week. Isn't it fortunate that she is *his* sister and not mine! He made me write at once and tell her that I would be out of Town for the whole of May. I *told* him it would never serve to hold her off, and of course it didn't. She wrote back immediately and said that she would be delighted to take charge of the household during my absence! So now poor Papa is having to put up at the Clarendon and at last I am to have all my cherished alterations put in hand. How many years have I spent in trying to persuade him?' And she hugged both sons impartially.

'Mama, you are a minx,' said Oliver fondly. 'Confess that you guessed how it would fall out!'

'Of course I did – and warned your father, too, but he wouldn't listen. So at last Aunt Arabella is made to serve a useful purpose, and my one regret is that I cannot be there myself to oversee the work.'

He smiled. 'Well, you are come in a very good hour. Do you not see that we have a visitor?'

Chantal dropped an embarrassed curtsey and wondered how to explain her presence and her unconventional appearance in a few brief words. A pair of wise and kindly eyes met hers.

'But I know you,' announced the lady in friendly fashion. 'You're the Delaney child, and grown almost out of recognition. What have you done with your shoes?' And then, in sudden concern, 'My dear girl! How *did* you come by that shocking bruise?'

'Just what I was about to explain to Oliver when you broke in on us,' said Dominic. 'Pray join our council of war, Mama. You may be able to suggest a solution to Lady Chantal's difficulties.'

But as she listened to the story, outlined by her son in laconic fashion wholly devoid of the melodramatic, her face grew more and more sober. It was a face that nature had designed to express joy, but much sorrow had warped its lines. With no claim to beauty, when its owner was happy it was wholly enchanting. In anxiety or grief, it fell all too easily into the lugubrious mask of the clown. For a moment Chantal was puzzled by an elusive resemblance. Then, on a hastily swallowed choke of laughter, realised that it was a resemblance to the hound, Jester.

'So I suggested that she should put up at

the White Hart for a day or two until we decide what is best to be done,' Dominic ended.

'Well that, at least, may be avoided,' said his mother soberly, 'now that I am come. You shall stay here, my child. You make light of the business, Dominic, but it is a very nasty one. Dangerous, too, I make no doubt.' She turned to Chantal and put out one slim hand to touch the girl's battered ones. 'I've no wish to alarm you, but it is better to face the truth. I am new come from Town and it is generally acknowledged that Roger Dickensen was murdered, though no one as yet has been able to suggest a motive. There was no robbery, you see, and he was not a man to make enemies. It could be' – the gentle hand clasped the girl's fingers – 'that his concern in your affairs has some bearing on the case, for from what you have suffered at your cousin's hands he seems to be a thorough-paced villain.'

'It is true that I would not put murder beyond him,' said Chantal quietly, 'but he has not left the Court these six weeks past, as I am all too well aware. He could not have compassed the deed himself.'

'I would not have expected him to do so.

He seems to be the sort of man who stands aside while others pull his chestnuts out of the fire. But it would be all too easy to procure a hired assassin. However, we waste our time on what can only be surmise. We must contrive a new identity for you. How many of the servants here have seen you?'

'I think only two of the grooms,' said Chantal, looking doubtfully at Dominic.

He nodded assent. 'But I'm afraid they would take particular notice,' he admitted ruefully. 'First because your appearance in itself is slightly unusual, and secondly because it is *highly* unusual for me to be driving any sort of female.'

His mother sighed. 'What a careless boy you are! You should have found some kind of disguise for her before you brought her home. Now we shall be forced to tell a great many lies, and I daresay they will prove our undoing, because I never can remember which particular story I preferred.' She nibbled one knuckle pensively while Chantal stared in some awe at a woman who could take a casual stranger under her wing, albeit in light-hearted fashion.

Presently the jester-face lit to amused enthusiasm. 'I have it,' she announced, 'and a simple enough tale, too. You shall be the naughty little daughter of a friend of mine. You have run away from the strict Grandmama with whom you were placed after some social faux pas – no need to make up a tale about that, I shall just draw a sober mouth and say that it is better forgotten. An escape from your bedroom by a conveniently placed tree will explain the loss of your shoes, and we can only hope the servants were incapable of distinguishing between a dressing gown and the latest high kick of fashion. I have come seeking you, your Mama being prostrated by this latest naughtiness, and am relieved to discover that you have fallen in with my son, who is, of course, well known to you. I shall attend to the matter of your wardrobe myself. The servants will believe that I brought your clothes with me from Town. Dominic, you shall escort me on a shopping expedition at once.' She quelled any possible objections to this suggestion before they could find utterance. Fixing her indignant son with a minatory eye, she said gently, 'Have you never heard, my son, that when you save a person's life, they become your responsibility? You, my child,' she turned her attention to Chantal, 'shall retire to your room – the Lilac room, I think, Oliver, next to mine – and repose yourself after your unpleasant experiences. And we must find another name for you. Your own is too distinctive.' She brooded over this for a moment, then said, 'Do you think you could remember to answer if we called you Janet, or Jan? I remember that your Papa spoke of you as his "little Shan", so it should not be too difficult. Yes?' And assuming Chantal's agreement she swept her off to her room, where she made notes of measurements and lists of necessities and brushed aside the girl's protests about the cost of the wardrobe that she deemed essential.

'You are well able to afford some pretty things,' she said firmly, 'and you will repay me when your affairs are settled. You will feel very much better when you are becomingly dressed. I shall not put you to the expense of a vast quantity of gowns, because your supposed naughtiness will furnish me with an excuse for not taking you about in local society. We don't entertain a great deal ourselves. Oliver finds large parties wearisome, while as for Dominic, I have only to suggest *any* kind of party and he promptly vanishes on one of his painting expeditions. So we shall be able to keep you close without attracting any particular notice.'

Which was all very well as a temporary measure, thought the slightly dazed 'Jan' when her kind hostess at last hurried off on her mission. But one could not lie hid for the better part of a year. She was fortunate to have fallen in with such kindly folk, but she could not possibly be such a charge on them. It was not just a question of money, though that was quite sufficiently embarrassing. It would be very wrong to expect strangers to devote their time and attention to her troubles. For tonight she would accept their generous hospitality, but there it must stop. By tomorrow she would be sufficiently restored to face her problems herself.

But when she joined the family for dinner that night, charmingly attired in a dress of amethyst-hued watered silk that was, she suspected, as expensive as it was becoming, she soon discovered that her new friends had quite other ideas. They dined very simply, and as soon as the servants had brought in the second course they were dismissed so that conversation could flow freely. Both gentlemen were full of ingenious schemes for keeping their young guest well hidden. These ranged from sending her on a feminine version of the grand tour to employing her as governess companion to their young cousin Helena, at present an unwilling pupil in a select seminary in Kensington.

Their mama listened indulgently, occasionally pointing out some circumstance that rendered a particular scheme ineligible, and presently announced firmly that this was all very entertaining but that she could see no reason why 'Jan' should not remain exactly where she was for the duration of her own visit. 'I shall be very glad of feminine society,' she said, smiling at Chantal, 'and since we live so retired it should be quite safe. When I go back to Town it will be a little more difficult. I think, then, it would be best for her to go to Dorne.'

There was a short silence as the brothers considered this suggestion. Oliver nodded thoughtfully. Dominic said, 'That's quite a sound notion, Mama, in some ways. Certainly I cannot call to mind any place that offers greater privacy, and I don't suppose Aunt Celia would mind. But Dorne is very isolated. If Lady – if 'Janet's' family *did* succeed in tracing her, it would be the simplest thing in the world for them to abduct her, and it could be days before we knew anything about it.'

'I was not suggesting that she should go alone,' said his mama placidly. 'She must be carefully guarded. Since it is two years since any of us were at Dorne, it would be a very suitable opportunity for *you* to visit Aunt Celia and assure yourself that she goes on comfortably. Murdoch is a very reliable steward but it is advisable for one of the family to look into matters from time to time. Oliver might like to go with you. The change of scene would be good for him – you were always very well at Dorne when you were a small boy,' she smiled tenderly at her elder son, 'and it would give Aunt Celia great pleasure to have you with her again.'

Chantal, glancing from face to face, noted the amused interest in Oliver's, the demure innocence of his mother's. Dominic's frown was only what she had expected. Naturally he would not want to spend his summer playing watch-dog to a foolish female who had already wasted far too much of his time. It was surprising, then, that before she could find words to reject the whole scheme, though with becoming gratitude, he should say, 'I don't see why it shouldn't be managed. Would you care for it, Noll?

The journey might be tedious, but the roads should be reasonable in June, and we needn't hurry ourselves. What do you say?'

'Rather, what does Lady Chantal say,' returned Oliver. 'I'm sorry, Mama. Jan, then. Though it is not near so pretty, besides seeming deuced familiar on such short acquaintance. It is asking a good deal, you know, to invite her to entrust herself to two strange gentlemen and their Aunt Celia who, darling though she is, is also, to put it mildly, a little eccentric. To live, moreover, on what amounts to a desert island which can only be reached by boat.'

'But that's the best part of it,' interrupted Dominic eagerly. 'The island bit. Easy to deny access to strangers. Murdoch dislikes them any way – says they disturb the birds and leave farm gates open. We could fish and sail and swim. I've been wanting to make some sketches of Dorne and this would be an ideal opportunity, while you, milord,' he grinned wickedly, 'can delve into estate matters with old Murdoch. An *excellent* scheme, Mama, and far more to my liking than to be spending the best weeks of the summer in Town, trailing from one intolerably dull party to the next'–

–'in attendance on no one more exciting

than your mama,' interrupted that lady with a gurgle of laughter. 'My *very* dear son! Always the essence of courtesy.'

She turned to Chantal with a shrug of laughing apology. 'Will you trust us, my dear? Though there is no need to make up your mind as yet. If the scheme mislikes you we have a whole month in which to devise something else.'

Chantal smiled back at her. 'Indeed I will,' she said simply. 'It sounds quite delightful. The more so' – she glanced thoughtfully at Dominic – 'since Mr. Merriden finds it appealing in itself and not just a safety measure taken in my interest. But will you not tell me more? Where *is* Dorne? The name has a familiar ring, yet I cannot exactly recall'–

There was a gleam of wary amusement in her hostess's eye. 'Dorne?' she said slowly, her gaze turning to Dominic, quizzing him unmercifully, 'It is our Scottish home. It is very small and rather inconvenient, being little more than an ancient castle perched on a rock with few modern comforts. My husband's youngest sister, Celia, lives there. She, too, is an artist, like my heedless son. I think she finds solace for the great loss that wrecked her life – her husband died in the retreat to Corunna – not only in her art, but by dwelling in the romantic past of her ancestors. As Oliver said, she is a darling, and I think you might come to love her dearly, but one is never quite sure which century she is living in, for she speaks of folk long dead as though they were dear familiar daily friends.' She hesitated for a moment, her glance turning from Chantal to Dominic, and back again, then went on resolutely, 'But small as it is, Dorne was the first seat of the Merridens, and my husband takes his title from it.'

So that was it. The careful avoidance of formal introductions; the vague hints that had teased her memory from time to time; the unobtrusive wealth, the very obvious arrogance, all were explained. The Marquess of Dorne. Of course she had heard of him, though Oliver's tragedy had occurred when she was a mere infant, been forgotten by the time that she made her debut. And Dominic– She coloured painfully as she recalled her foolish jibe about a great gentleman incognito. There, at least, he had been sensitive, considerate. Perhaps he had felt some embarrassment. Certainly he had made no parade of consequence.

At this juncture her hostess put an end to any possible awkwardness by giving the signal for the ladies to withdraw.

'Not that either of them cares overmuch for their wine,' she confided cheerfully as she led the way to the drawing room, 'But it will give my poor Dominic time to recover his countenance. Men are quite idiotish, aren't they? I guessed, when I heard you address him as Mr. Merriden, that he had boggled at telling you who he was. And it does make things awkward when you are expected to know all about a host of new acquaintances and actually you haven't an inkling. Pray forgive him. It isn't conceit, you know.'

'And I made matters worse,' confessed Chantal, appeased by this sympathetic attitude. 'In all the business of pulling me out of the water and awaiting my return to consciousness, it is scarcely surprising that he had not thought to tell me his name. And I'm afraid that I did not show a proper gratitude for his services. Forgive me, ma'am, but his manners are *not* conciliatory, and though he did all that was needful for my comfort he made it very plain that I was a pesky nuisance. Since my own temper is not of the meekest, we were soon at outs, and I flung some cheap jibe at him about the behaviour proper to a gentleman which made it impossible for him to admit his rank without sounding like an out and out coxcomb. The confusion was quite as much my fault as his.'

Her hostess said gently, 'That is generous in you. It is never easy for a mother to admit to any fault in her child, however plainly she may see it. But now that the situation is resolved, let us consider your case a little more closely. It is all very well, you know, for you to stay here just now, and I was quite sincere when I said that I would enjoy feminine society. My sons are darlings and I love them dearly, but men are not very conversible, are they? But though you will, I trust, be safe enough here, and pass the summer in similar fashion at Dorne, you cannot lurk in hiding for ever. Something must be done to scotch this absurd rumour about your sanity.' The Marchioness of Dorne was not one to shy at an ill-sounding word. 'Yes. I had heard of it. And disbelieved it, my family and yours having been well acquainted for generations past. I knew you only by sight, but your parents I knew well, and there was nothing in your breeding to give substance to such a tale. It must be dealt with legally. The boys may have their romantic notions of defending you and challenging all your enemies. It will amuse them and may serve very well for a time, but it cannot endure. I think you should write to Mr. Dickensen's partner, explaining the persecution to which you have been subjected and how you have only just learned of the rumours that are being spread. Tell him that you have taken shelter with us for the time being, but insist that *no one* is to be furnished with your direction on any pretext whatever.'

Chantal found this sensible suggestion distinctly comforting. And when her hostess went on to speak of her father and of the mother she could not remember she began to feel, as she was meant to feel, that she was with friends of long standing, no longer an intruder or a nuisance. For the first time since her father's death she found herself speaking freely about him to someone other than Hepsie. She talked of Hepsie, too, and of her concern for the old woman's fate. 'For there are none of the old servants left who were there in my father's time,' she explained, 'though the little maid who waited on us seemed kindly enough.' And at last, drawn out by skilful and sympathetic handling, she spoke of her father's death and of the manner of it, pouring out all the hideous details that her cousin had told her.

The marchioness listened to this part of the story with a horrified revulsion that matched Chantal's own. 'I don't believe it!' she declared stoutly. 'Had it been so, some word of it must have been generally known. And there was not so much as a whisper. I believe the whole thing is an invention of your cousin's, deliberately planned to distress you so that you would shrink from a return to normal living.'

Chantal looked at her in mingled doubt and hope. 'Is there any way we could find out?' she asked. 'His death I could accept, for he died as a soldier would wish, in the service of his country. I need not hide it now. The expedition was designed to discover the extent of Russian influence in Afghanistan. My father was invited to join it because he knew the country well, having served in India for many years under Lord Wellesley. He explained this to me himself. It is only the thought that he might have suffered so horribly that I find unendurable.'

'Those who planned the expedition must know the truth. They may be reluctant to admit responsibility openly but I am sure it should be possible to set your mind at rest. I shall write to my husband and see what he can discover for us. But here come our tardy gentlemen – after I gave them such good characters, too. I'm ashamed of you both – succumbing to the lure of the grape when we have such a charming visitor.'

'No such thing, Mama,' defended Dominic promptly, as he steered the wheelchair over to the hearth where the two ladies were sitting. 'In fact we have been engaged in the service of that same guest. We have been in the library studying the best route for our journey north. I trust that *you* have succeeded in persuading her that Dorne will be a secure refuge.'

'Oh, she has no doubts about that,' announced his mother. 'But we had best warn the poor child exactly what she is in for before she commits herself to the venture. Do you take her to the library, my dear, and show her Celia's sketches of the place and such maps as we possess, while I enjoy a comfortable cose with Oliver.'

Oliver twinkled down at her as the door closed behind his brother. 'Don't overplay your hand, Mama,' he cautioned. 'That was a little too obvious.'

'I'm afraid it was,' she agreed guiltily. 'But I was so pleased. She is the first girl to whom Dominic has paid any attention since you were hurt.'

'I daresay. But his attentions are not of an amatory nature, you know. Which is perhaps as well. Her reputation scarcely recommends her as a possible bride for him – not, certainly, in my father's eyes. If one believes even half the tales that are told of her, she is wickedly extravagant and wild to a fault.'

'That I do *not* believe. Why! She would have chided me for extravagance in my buying if gratitude and good breeding had not forbade. As to her outrageous exploits – at least they were never sordid nor underhanded. And no man's name was ever coupled with hers. But if she succeeds only in curing Dominic of his warped distrust of women, I shall be more than satisfied. She does not have to marry him,' she conceded kindly.

Oliver laughed outright. 'That, too, is perhaps fortunate. She is very lovely, which would probably appeal to his artist's eye, but if I'm any judge she has a will of her own and a temper, too. That would never do for Nick, who is fiery enough for two. I should think something clinging and sweetly docile would be more to his taste.'

His mother eyed him thoughtfully. 'You may be right,' she said gently. 'At least we shall have all summer in which to find out.'

Four

'Jan tells me that this is yours,' said the marchioness, handing Dominic a neatly folded crimson silk wrapper.

He took it from her, frowning. 'Do we have to call her by that absurd name?' he said abruptly. 'Surely there is no one here to carry tales to her cousin. It makes me feel like a stage conspirator. I shall never remember.'

'Which is why you must practise now, where there *is* no one to carry tales. Think of the long journey north. You must lie overnight at half a dozen different inns, as well as stopping to change horses and to refresh yourselves at twice as many more. A name so unusual, carelessly dropped, could betray you all. Some curious fellow traveller has only to mention to his acquaintance that he met the Marquess of Dorne's sons escorting a Lady Chantal something or other on a journey north, and there is an end of your fine plan. At the moment I am more interested in *this* exotic garment. I do not think I am, in general, a prying parent, but for once I confess to a certain degree of curiosity.'

Her son eyed the incriminating garment blandly. 'That? Oh – I rather think Kate must have left it behind. Or was it Lucy? Yes it looks more Lucy's style. It was fortunate that I had it by me, wasn't it?'

His parent regarded him severely. 'You may gammon Oliver with your taradiddles,' she informed him with regrettable vulgarity, 'but don't try to come that game on me. I know you too well. Would you care to tell me the truth, or am I to believe that you bought this exceedingly feminine garment for your own use?'

He laughed and hugged her. 'Very well, Mama, but I'm afraid you won't like the truth any better than my taradiddles. I bought it for the colour.'

She tapped her foot impatiently. He said carefully, 'It is a very difficult colour to paint, and I wanted to get it absolutely right, which can only be done if you have the actual fabric before you.'

'Do you really expect me to believe that you meant to paint a picture of a dressing gown?'

'Well no. There is a little more to it than

that,' he admitted. 'Do you remember last summer, when Aunt Arabella was for ever teasing me to paint Helena's portrait? I consented at last for the sake of peace.' His lips twitched slightly but he went on solemnly enough, 'I had it in mind to paint her as a Spanish gipsy. A Catalan, I thought. They are very picturesque, you know, and Helena's colouring would have lent itself admirably to such a personification. Unfortunately the wretched child took the measles, so the whole scheme came to nothing. But I kept the wrapper in case Aunt Arabella had thoughts of reviving it.'

'What an odious wretch you are,' said his mother placidly. 'You know perfectly well that Helena's olive skin and black hair are the greatest trial to her mama, with the rest of the family so golden fair. I can only regard the measles as a merciful dispensation of Providence.'

'Aunt Arabella is a very stupid woman,' said her son dispassionately. 'She should know better than to try to bully me into painting portraits, which is not my métier. As for Helena, she will be a handsome creature when she matures a little and will shine down the insipid blondes. Her eyes are particularly fine. What's more she is a nice child. She would have enjoyed being a gipsy.'

'Jan has beautiful eyes, too,' his mother said.

He nodded indifferently. 'Yes. And doubtless knows well enough how to use them to lure some poor fool into the honey trap.' And then, relenting a little, 'Not that she has shown us *that* side of her nature.'

'If she has such a side,' said his mother rather indignantly. 'To me there is too much sadness in her face, though a great deal of sweetness, too. Oliver has taken a marked liking to her, though he was very dubious at first, knowing her reputation. Poor child! She is much to be pitied. Had her mother lived she would never have been permitted to run wild as she did.'

'But then she would not have been Chantal,' said Dominic unexpectedly. And his mama was so interested by the new note in his voice that she forebore to correct him. 'Surely her honesty and her straight thinking are the result of her father's training, as is her courage,' he went on reflectively. And with considerable self restraint the marchioness refrained from telling him that it was perfectly possible for a mother, too, to be honest and brave and clear minded. Instead she asked at what hour he proposed to set out for Town, as she had not yet finished her letter to her husband.

'And you have Jan's letter safe?' she added. 'It was well thought of that you should take it to her attorney's in person. One would not care to have some officious underling reading of her difficulties.'

He agreed absently, told her that he would be leaving in about an hour's time if that would be convenient for her, though there was no particular haste now that daylight lasted so long, and strolled off to the library to enquire if Oliver had any commissions for him to execute in Town.

He found his brother playing chess with Jan – as he must remember to call her – and, for a brief moment felt almost an intruder, so intent where the two on their game. Or perhaps it would be more accurate to say that Jan was intent. Oliver was leaning back in his chair, an indulgent grin on his face, while Jan, chin on fist, the summer sun that streamed through the oriel window lighting her hair to a fleeting chestnut glory, was creasing slender dark brows over an impossible situation. She was not even aware of Dominic's approach as she said, 'Oh! Very well, then. Black resigns. It is useless, you know. Papa always said that chess was a man's game. It requires masculine logic and a military appreciation of tactics.'

Oliver smiled. 'If that is true you play far too good a game for a woman. There is no chivalry left in me. I am put to all shifts to defeat you. Now I'll tell you what we shall do. While Dominic is in Town I'll teach you one or two tricks that may deceive him. He prides himself on his game – can rarely be persuaded to play his poor invalid brother – and it would do him a great deal of good to suffer defeat at your hands. What do you say?'

'That your remarks are nothing short of slanderous,' interrupted Dominic promptly. 'How many times have you declined my suggestion of a game, proclaiming that it was a dead bore? But now that you have a pretty opponent whom you can defeat without undue exertion, you are all alacrity. Short sport, brother, short sport! When I come back from Town, it is not Jan who will receive my challenge, but my poor invalid brother!'

Chantal usually found the exchanges between the brothers of absorbing interest. Herself an only child, the lazy banter that passed between them, the occasional hot argument, which generally ended with neither conceding a single point but both perfectly good humoured about it, and the unobtrusive consideration that each showed for the other's welfare, were a completely new experience and an attractive one. But on this occasion she was so startled to hear herself described as pretty by an avowed misogynist that she missed the end of the argument.

An even greater shock was in store. During the week that had passed since her arrival at Claverton she had ridden out once or twice, either with Dominic or escorted by one of the grooms. She and her hostess were of much the same build. Riding demurely side-saddle in a sober borrowed habit, her new guardians hoped that no one would recognise the dashing Lady Chantal Delaney. She must have *some* fresh air and exercise and should be safe enough so long as she kept to unfrequented byways. No comment had been made on her excellent horsemanship though the truth of the matter was that she rode just as well side-saddle as astride, and only foolish caprice had led her to adopt the masculine mode. So she was completely taken by surprise when Dominic, having noted down one or two items that Oliver wanted, turned to her and said politely, 'I would be much obliged to you, ma'am, if you could spare the time to exercise Pegeen for me while I am away. I may be gone ten days or so, and the foolish creature frets for me. She seems to have taken a fancy to you, and I can trust you not to spoil her mouth.'

She managed to stammer a few rather disjointed phrases expressive of pleasure at the suggestion, and to bid him farewell in a slightly more collected manner, but the face that she turned to Oliver as the door closed behind his brother was so full of amazement that he laughed outright.

'It was indeed a great compliment,' he told her, 'but no need to look quite so shocked. Nick is no fool. He may have little use for women, but he dotes on Pegeen. Only the best is good enough for her. He told me after your first ride together that you had the best seat and the lightest hands of anyone he knew. He wouldn't permit his foolish prejudice to influence his judgement in such a matter.'

Chantal shook her head in puzzled fashion. 'I shall never understand him,' she said. And then, tentatively, 'Had it been you who took females in such dislike, it would have been reasonable enough.'

Oliver said gently, 'If you give it a little more thought, I think you may see it from Dominic's point of view. When you are much attached to someone, it is hard to see them suffer. Harder, I think, than to suffer yourself. If only you could share the suffering – take some part of the burden. And of course it can't be done. Dominic does all he can – and far more than he should – to make my life full and pleasant, but that is not quite the same thing. And he was at a very impressionable age when I was struck down. At first he seemed actually to resent his own strength and vigour, seeing me so helpless, and would not indulge in any of the active pursuits that we had shared. In fact that did me more good than all the doctors' treatments, for I *had* to make an effort for his sake. Gradually I persuaded him to go riding and climbing and sailing again, on the plea that he could bring back sketches and stories of what he had done so that we could share them. When he discovered that I could still swim and sail and fish with him I think his delight equalled my own. At Dorne you will see him at his best, for when we go on these expeditions he tends and guards me as fiercely as any lion his cubs. At first, you see, I could not endure to have anyone stare at my useless limbs. If you are to make one of our party, be very careful not to betray either shock or pity. I am glad to have had this opportunity of speaking with you so frankly. If you can bring yourself to treat me exactly as though I was a normal man, you could do much to rid him of his prejudice. It was the thought that any woman should reject his much-loved big brother that began it.'

'Yes. That I can understand. And the bit about watching a dear one suffer and being helpless. Thank you for explaining. As for exhibiting shock or pity, my first thought on meeting you was that you didn't look in the least invalidish. Besides, pity will do no good, will it? To clasp my hands and weep for your sad case could only depress both of us. Far better if I can make you laugh and keep you entertained.'

He looked amused. 'Which you do to admiration,' he told her with a little bow. 'In fact I am fast coming round to the belief that your unusual up-bringing – for which, no doubt, the world either pities or condemns you, according to its degree of Christian charity – has much to commend it.'

This conversation carried them several paces along the road to an easy relationship. Since the marchioness, too, had been pleasantly impressed by Chantal's transparent honesty and by the touch of diffidence so unexpected in one who bore the reputation of being a 'fast little piece' the three of them settled down very comfortably together. It was not long before the Merridens reached the conclusion that the girl's reputation was largely undeserved. Where matters of principle or delicacy of feeling were concerned, she was 'as sound as a roast,' Oliver informed his mother.

She nodded. 'Yes. I fancy she grew up trying to be the son that her father had wanted. Her faults are those of a headstrong stripling, eager to prove that he can deal as capably as his elders. It's scarcely surprising. Her earliest years were spent with her grandmother, a formidable old termagant who petrified most adults. Goodness knows how she appeared in the eyes of a child, but certainly she took such pride in her high breeding that she held herself to be above the rulings of convention, a belief which doubtless she would instil into her granddaughter. When her papa succeeded to the title and sold out, he took Chantal to live with him. But since he admired her courage and her high spirits he never tried to check her wilful ways and showed his affection by showering her with every luxury. She has never been disciplined and she has never known tenderness. Well – life itself has taken a hand in the matter of discipline. It is for us to show her the kindness, the consideration for her comfort, that will help her through this trying time. And it isn't difficult. For my part I find her very loveable.'

So it was that when Dominic came back he found his protégée very much at home – so much a member of the family that it almost seemed as though she had been born into it. His days in Town had been crammed with business and social engagements consequent upon the change in his summer plans. There had been no time for speculating as to how his family were adjusting to the presence of the waif he had foisted on to them. It was only as he resigned the reins to his groom and strolled up to the house in search of refreshment that he spared a thought for the sort of welcome that might await him. It proved to be not at all what he had expected.

In the library he drew blank. Moreover the familiar room had an oddly bare, unused look. Further search discovered his mother stretched on a day-bed in her boudoir absorbed in a novel, and upon enquiry he learned that Chantal and his brother were out in the garden.

'It seems that Jan knows nothing about fishing,' explained his mother placidly, 'so Oliver has undertaken to instruct her in the gentle art of casting a fly.'

'*Oliver* has!' exclaimed Dominic.

'Why, yes. These last three days, since it has been so fine. And vows she is making good progress. She is a delightful girl, Dominic, and the change she has wrought in Oliver is almost unbelievable. I begin to feel that it really was Providence that cast her in your way. Do you know that he actually permits her to push his chair about the grounds? And twice he has driven out with her in the gig. Only about the lanes, of course, but since *she* could not venture into the city she begged the pleasure of his company so that he might tell her about the farms and villages and places of local interest. He looks so much gayer and younger. But you will see for yourself. Tell me. Have you made any progress towards settling Jan's affairs?'

'Only that I had no difficulty in convincing Parker – he is, or should I say *was* the junior partner in Dickensen's firm – of the truth of my tale. But as he pointed out, the conspiracy is difficult to prove. No one, at this stage, can precisely recall who first started the rumours about Chantal's sanity. If the authorities should apprehend the thugs who murdered Dickensen, something might be done, especially if it proved possible to link them with her unpleasant cousin. One thing is sure. Parker will make every effort to see that they are brought to justice. He seems to have been devoted to the old man, and is hot for vengeance. Meanwhile he approves our plans for Chantal. He suggested that he should furnish her with funds so that she need not feel herself a charge on us, and I accepted, knowing that she felt her financial dependence irksome. He assures me that her relatives will not dare to demand an accounting, since they cannot produce her person. I daresay he is right. He seemed an uncommonly sensible fellow.'

His mother was less complaisant. 'I daresay he is right in that particular,' she agreed doubtfully, 'and certainly Jan will be much happier with money in her purse. But we cannot hide her forever and until the business is cleared up she must be dreadfully uneasy, not knowing how her enemies are moving against her. Can nothing more be done?'

Her son eyed her thoughtfully. 'Not legally, Mama,' he said gently. 'Chantal would never, I am convinced, choose to bring an action against them. It is only her word against theirs – and think of the scandal! Parker says that sooner or later they must make some move to trace her whereabouts. If they succeed in doing so, we shall be ready for them.'

She was in no wise reassured, but judged it better to let matters rest there. 'And the other business? Was your father able to discover anything about the manner of the Earl's death?'

'Yes. And mightily indignant that anyone should put such lies about. Not a syllable of truth in those grisly details that so distressed the poor brat. He was clean killed – shot through the heart. Nor was there any mutilation, though I daresay there might have been had not the main party come up quickly. It seems such practices are fashionable in those parts, so there was a basis of truth for the lie. You will be pleased that you can set her mind at rest.'

His mother sighed thankfully and suggested that when he had rid himself of the grime of travel he should go in search of the missing pair and remind them that tea would be served on the terrace in about half an hour. 'For I put dinner back an hour, not expecting you to make such good speed.'

He found them by the bank of the tiny stream that fed the water gardens, and between the song of the water and their own laughter they did not hear his approach.

'It's better. But you're still using your wrist too much. Try to remember to use the whole of your forearm. And that one landed downstream.' Thus Oliver.

Chantal's rod came back for another cast. Dominic recognised it as the one that his brother had used as a schoolboy, well suited in length and weight to his present pupil. The cast was better this time, the line falling lightly on the water and the fly floating down towards the angler in the desired fashion.

'Excellent,' approved Oliver.

She turned a glowing face towards him. The tip of the rod described a neat arc, the line entangled itself in a willow tree that grew beside the stream, and pleasure turned to dismay as Chantal perceived Dominic's tall figure behind his brother's. She blushed furiously. Why must his lordship always appear just when she had made a fool of herself? But she smiled gaily enough, even as she said penitently to Oliver, 'There, milord. That's a female for you. No concentration – and after the times you have warned me! This is even worse than chess.'

Oliver laughed. 'But it was a beautiful cast. So long as you don't forget to reel in when you strike into a fish, I may yet be proud of my pupil.' He worked his chair over to the tree and helped her to free the line.

Dominic said, 'Mama sent me to call you to tea.' And then, quizzically, 'Have you had good sport, ma'am?'

There was a flash in the grey eyes that were bent on the tangled line. 'First-rate, I thank you, milord. I have given the minnows a dreadful fright. One of them was quite two inches long – the poor thing turned quite pale when it saw my determined efforts. Fortunately the enjoyment of sport depends on the company one keeps, rather than on the size of the catch,' she ended tartly, and began to take down her rod.

Dominic grinned. He had asked for that, since he knew very well that there were no fish in the tiny stream, and was rather amused that the chit should put him in his place so promptly. By way of amends he came forward to help her. Oliver commented favourably on the speed he must have made from Town and asked how he had left their father, and the brief brangle was over.

Privately Chantal regretted her impulsive riposte. He had only been joking her. From Oliver she accepted such teasing in good part. Indeed she recognised it as a compliment of no mean order. Why should she resent it from his brother? Gratitude alone should enable her to endure indignities worse than a little teasing without complaint, yet it seemed as though they could never meet without sparks flying. And that final pointed remark about keeping good company had been rude. She had meant it so at the time, but now she was sorry. Over the tea table she was unwontedly subdued, wondering if she should apologise or whether that would be making too much of a trivial incident.

To complete her discomfiture, the marchioness took the first opportunity of acquainting her with the tidings that Dominic had brought from Town. The true account of her father's death brought her a peace of mind that she had not known for a year. She shed a few foolish tears and was patted and soothed to calmness in a motherly way that was very comfortable. The information that she could now draw upon her own funds for necessary expenses was also received with relief. Her hostess brushed lightly over Mr. Parker's other remarks, saying only that he fully approved the notion of going to Dorne, and then said amusedly, 'Dominic has been very busy in your behalf. You should be flattered. I daresay he has not so bestirred himself for a woman in the whole of his life.'

Chantal stared at her in dismay. 'Oh dear! And I was quite shockingly rude to him,' she exclaimed.

'Were you, my dear? Do tell me,' said Dominic's unnatural mama.

She chuckled over the faltering recital and assured the girl that her son was not one to take a pet for so small a matter. In fact, she added shrewdly, it had probably amused him, and possibly even provided him with a much needed lesson. 'For he is apt to address all females as though they are either still in the nursery or half-witted,' she explained serenely, 'and it is high time that he learned better. Believe me, my dear, I am positively grateful to you for extending his education in this respect.'

If Chantal could not take quite such a light-hearted view of her own behaviour she was a little comforted, though she was still resolved to mend matters at the first opportunity.

This occurred after dinner, when Dominic, following his usual custom, strolled out on to the terrace to smoke a cigar, a habit deeply deplored by his mama. Chantal excused herself to her hostess and followed him. He turned at the sound of her footsteps and awaited her coming. Being Chantal she went straight to the point without preamble.

'I wanted to thank you, milord, for the trouble you have taken over my wretched affairs. For going to see Mr. Parker yourself and for arranging about money matters, but most of all for your enquiries about my father. Indeed I should thank you for *all* your kindness to me since chance threw me in your path, and it ill beseems me to be ripping up at you as I did this afternoon. For that I beg your pardon.'

Dominic badly wanted to laugh. The shy, stiff little voice made her sound like a seven-year-old with a lesson well conned. He said politely, 'You make too much of it, ma'am. Since I had to be in Town any way, it cost me small pains to deliver your letter myself.

Mama and I were agreed that it would be foolish to risk its falling into the wrong hands. As for the other enquiries – it is my father who deserves your thanks. He has a wide acquaintance in government circles and knew just the man to approach. May I, however, say that it has given me much pleasure to be the bearer of more comfortable tidings. It would make me even happier if I could also give your dear cousin his due deserts. But that, alas, seems unlikely, since it is an object with us to avoid an encounter with him at this present.'

He did not refer to her apology, and for this she was grateful. It was, after all, so small a matter. They took a turn or two about the terrace, Dominic speaking of the arrangements to be set in hand for their journey north in so interesting and sensible a fashion that any lingering embarrassment was banished and she found herself actually liking him very well.

Five

This comfortable state of affairs was not destined to last. Coming into the library next morning to see if Oliver was ready to go out with her, Chantal found him seated at a desk piled high with papers.

He gave her his attractive twisted grin. 'Sorry, m'dear. One or two matters in this little lot need prompt attention. Will you hold me excused this morning? No need to forego your lesson. Here is my idle brother with no better employment on hand. He may very well tend to your instruction. And to do him justice he is a better practitioner with rod and line than ever I was.'

It seemed to Chantal manifestly unfair that one brother should spend this lovely morning wrestling with musty old papers while the other disported himself in the sunshine. She accompanied Dominic obediently but a tiny frown creased her brow as she considered what seemed to her a very idle existence.

Dominic said resignedly, 'Now what's

amiss? For well I know when you wear that Friday face that I have done something to displease your ladyship.'

She had not thought herself so transparent. But since he had asked, he might as well hear the truth.

'Could you not have helped your brother with his work?' she said stiffly.

'I could,' he retorted, 'but I have no intention of doing so. It is estate business and no concern of mine.'

The tone implied that it was no concern of hers either. She flushed hotly, but refused to be so easily silenced. 'It is strange to find two brothers so different in temperament,' she told him meditatively.

'You find us so?'

'Your brother is so conscientious; so wholly devoted to the Merriden interest, while you seem to care little for it. You must know how happy it would make your mama if you were to marry and set up your nursery, besides giving your father the comfort of seeing the succession secure.'

'If ever I find another woman the equal of mama, I might even be cajoled into matrimony,' he said indifferently. 'As for the succession, you are talking nonsense. There are several broods of cousins littering the countryside, so there is no cause for anxiety.'

Still she persisted. 'Surely you must have some feeling for your home. For the lands that Merridens have held for centuries and for the people who have served your family for generation after generation?'

He seemed to give this some consideration. 'I am fond of *this* place,' he agreed judicially. 'And both Oliver and I are much attached to Dorne, which is any small boy's idea of Paradise. But Merriden Castle, my father's principal seat, is quite hideously ugly, as well as shockingly inconvenient. Were you picturing it as some romantic Gothic survival? Nothing of the sort, I assure you. As for the tenantry' – the light casual voice was suddenly serious – 'I do not concern myself with them. It is Oliver who is my father's heir. He can never hope to walk or ride over the lands that will one day be his. But he can drive out to visit his tenants, discuss their problems and listen to their views. On paper he can know every field – what crops will do well, whether the soil is rich or poor or subject to flood, a dozen different details that will serve to endear him to his people. Would you have me take over the one thing that he can do superlatively well?'

She was silenced – indeed abashed, for she could see exactly what he meant. She turned impulsively to express her regret for so misjudging him, but the lean, hard face looked so cold, so forbidding, that the words died on her lips. She murmured rather foolishly, 'No. Of course you could not. I had not thought of it like that,' and wondered once more why this man must always put her in the wrong or find her in some foolish predicament. It aroused in her a slightly ridiculous determination to show at her best under his tuition.

Alas! Determination is not conducive to ease and flexibility. After half a dozen disastrous casts she was hot and angry and very much inclined to blame her tutor, who was wisely restricting his advice to a minimum. She said crossly, 'What am I doing wrong? I've never been so clumsy before, not even the first day.'

'Your stance is not quite right,' he said carefully, 'and you are holding the rod with your thumb curled round it instead of extended along the butt. See – like this.'

He came to stand behind her and placed the fingers and thumb of her right hand in the correct position. Then, with his left hand grasping her shoulder and his right closed firmly over hers, he made several trial casts, so that she could catch the rhythm of the movements.

Standing so, Chantal was vividly conscious of the warmth of his body, of the strength in the hands that held her so firmly yet so impersonally. To her later shame and fury, an unusual surge of feeling swept through her, a longing to lean back against his shoulder and feel those powerful arms close round her.

It lasted only a moment. Then she said rather breathlessly, 'I think I have it now. May I try again?' And was released.

Fortunately the next two or three casts were rather better, and presently she was able to lay aside the rod and say that she had had enough for the time being. She must change her dress, she explained, since she meant to drive out with his mother; and was able to withdraw from the scene of that curious experience in reasonably good order.

She could not, however, put it out of her mind quite so easily. She had only to recall the circumstances to feel some faint resurgence of the longing that had shaken her. There was no understanding it, for she did not even *like* Dominic Merriden above half. So she was at considerable pains to find some explanation for her shameful reaction to his proximity. But it was not until she was making ready for bed that it came to her. Of course! Lonely and apprehensive as she inevitably was, despite the kindness of her new friends, instinct was bidding her seek some safe anchorage. What more natural, then, than that she should turn to Dominic, the very epitome of strength and careless vigour?

She sighed her relief that she had not, after all, succumbed to a foolish passion for a wholly unresponsive gentleman, blew out her candle and snuggled down between the sheets.

It was easy enough to maintain this comfortable self-deception during the remainder of her stay at Claverton. There was much to be done in preparation for a prolonged sojourn in what, the marchioness warned her, was a very isolated spot. No one could rely on a summer of unbroken fine weather, and some provision must be made for wet days. Chantal must select all the books she might need from the library, for there was none worth the mention at Dorne. Anything that she required for her embroidery must be bought in Bath, and Dominic undertook to purchase a selection of music by her favourite composers. Though there was no library at Dorne, there was a music room which the family used on all informal occasions instead of the rather prim drawing room. All of them were musical in an amateur fashion and many a leisurely evening was beguiled in listening to Oliver's violin or Dominic's singing.

'Which makes it particularly fortunate that you are such an accomplished pianist,' added Lady Dorne happily.

Chantal was a little startled by the size of the cavalcade that was eventually assembled for the journey. She had realised that special provision would have to be made for Oliver's comfort, but the extent of that provision surprised her. The travelling coach had been built to order by one of Longacre's foremost craftsmen. Wide doors permitted the wheel chair to be lifted in and strapped into position beside a single seat facing the horses. For much of the journey Chantal occupied that seat, though Oliver urged her to ride whenever the weather was favourable.

'For you are not to be sitting mewed up in a stuffy carriage all day in attendance on a crotchety cripple,' he told her firmly.

Sometimes Dominic came to join them but mostly he preferred to ride, so Oliver was Chantal's chief companion, and an agreeable one she found him, well-informed without being boringly garrulous.

The marchioness had gone back to Town, with many promises of letters to be exchanged and a possible visit to Dorne in August. 'You can stay there very comfortably until September is out,' she had said. 'Perhaps your affairs will be settled by then. My husband and I will do our utmost to hasten matters but obviously we must move with caution for fear of betraying your whereabouts.'

Chantal was in the mood to be hopeful about the future. A month of freedom from the unnatural strain of the past year had restored her spirits as much as good food had revitalised her body, and she was once again the eager vigorous creature that nature had intended.

On the last two or three evenings at Claverton she had worn some of her prettiest new gowns, on the pretext that there would be small opportunity of wearing them at Dorne. She had looked quite delightfully, the sheen of health once more on hair and skin, and Oliver had immediately entered a strong objection to her remarks about wearing the dresses.

'We are not savages, you know, even if we do hail from north of the border. Think of my brother's artistic eye and the pleasure that your appearance must give him! Perhaps if we have made a long day's excursion we may be lazy and dress informally, but if the weather keeps us indoors, then Nick and I will change into evening rig and you must do so too. Then we can feast our eyes on beauty and our ears on music,' he added with one of his comical little bows.

The gentleman with the artistic eye did not endorse his brother's suggestion but neither did he object to the prospect of being obliged to change his dress for dinner when he was supposedly rusticating. The marchioness, studying his impassive countenance, wondered how long he would hold out against this enchanting young creature who was blossoming before their eyes. If he did not succumb before the summer was out, then she would indeed despair of him.

They took a fortnight over the journey. It could have been accomplished in half the time, but they did not hurry, and they made a wide detour to spend a couple of nights at

Merriden. Dominic said it would do them all good to have a rest from the continual jounce and sway of the carriage, and that he wanted to show Jan just how accurately he had described the place.

At the outset Chantal had wondered how they would ever find accommodation for so large a party. Since the month was June, the most favoured month of all for those who must travel, inns were likely to be crowded. She foresaw considerable discomfort. She was to discover how much wealth and good organisation could do to smooth the way. Couriers had been sent ahead to engage rooms, to arrange for changes of horses, even to order tempting meals. The travellers had nothing to do but enjoy the passing scene and each other's society. She was reluctantly obliged to concede that once again she had underestimated Lord Dominic's capabilities. Even though it had secured her comfort she found herself resenting his efficiency.

The first day had seemed very long. By the time they reached Gloucester she was heartily sick of the confinement of the coach and thankful to submit to the ministrations of the comfortable abigail whom the marchioness had selected as her attendant.

'She'll not be able to dress your hair in the latest mode or advise you as to fashion's newest quirks,' that lady had warned, 'but if you are travel-sick or take a feverish cold she will know just what to do.'

Tonight Chantal had good cause to bless the marchioness's forethought. Hilda was deft and placid. It was a refreshed and well-groomed girl who presently joined the gentlemen for dinner.

They were apologetic for the boredom that she had been required to endure. At least Oliver was. Dominic said only that he felt they might now consider themselves safe from recognition and, this being so, might venture to look about the city next day. Chantal, who had never chanced to visit it before, welcomed the suggestion eagerly. The cathedral was particularly fine, he told her, and the remains of the old city walls would doubtless appeal to a female with sentimental yearnings for days long past.

The morning's strolling exploration set the pattern for many which were to follow. Oliver, sensitive over his disabilities, did not accompany them, but was ready to lend an interested ear to Chantal's animated account of all that they had seen and appeared to share her sentiments more fully than his brother. They lunched early and set off on the next stage of their journey – a short one this time, a mere twenty miles through the vale of Evesham. They lay that night at Evesham itself and spent the next morning in exploration of the little town gazing respectfully at the site of the battle on Green Hill and appreciatively at the beautiful old Bell Tower.

Another short stage took them to Stratford-on-Avon. Chantal, suspecting that they were deliberately dawdling for her pleasure when they would rather have pressed on to Dorne, taxed them with indulging her more than was reasonable. Oliver looked guilty and murmured something rather unconvincing about short stages being better for *him*. Dominic, brushing aside the halting phrases, said coolly, 'Nothing of the kind. We are merely attending to the sad gaps in your education. Who was it who thought "Measure for Measure" was a Sheridan comedy? Well – we are coming into Shakespeare country now – shall actually pass through the Forest of Arden. Can you, my little ignoramus, tell us which of the bard's plays uses Arden as its setting?'

Chantal had no idea – but she forgot all about her well founded reproaches. And she was too wise to indulge in rash guesses. 'If we are to talk of ignorance,' she retorted with spirit, 'who was it who had never heard of Simon de Montfort or the battle of Evesham?'

Dominic grinned. '*That* swashbuckling revolutionary? A fellow of very dubious moral character, too, if I am to believe what I read in that very interesting book that you so obligingly pressed upon me. I'd be willing to wager a handsome sum that he seduced the king's sister in order to force Henry's consent to the marriage. I cannot understand your admiration for such a villain.'

Chantal flushed hotly. Simon de Montfort was her particular hero. Where others of her friends had admired Richard Coeur de Lion or the Black Prince, some quirk of imagination had fixed her girlish devotion on the long dead Earl of Leicester. Dominic's charges might well be justified, but Earl Simon had captured her fancy. If *she* had been King Henry's sister– She blushed more hotly than ever and said furiously, 'At least he was a man. He didn't just sneer and criticise other people and do nothing. He loved and he fought and he lost and he died, but he lived his life to the full.'

There was a horrid little silence. Then

Oliver said mildly, 'If you two have done arguing over de Montfort, perhaps we may return to Master Shakespeare. *There* is what is left of the Forest of Arden, Jan.' He gestured towards it. 'As for Earl Simon, perhaps I should warn you that there is some vague connection between our families. Possibly some of that warrior blood flows in *our* veins. Not that I have ever bothered to trace the relationship, but Mama, who seems to share your predilection for these fire-eaters, has frequently boasted of it. A pity that you must make do with his milk-and-water off-shoots, but I daresay you will find them much more comfortable to live with. All that armour, you know.'

Which made both contestants laugh and so served the speaker's purpose admirably.

They dawdled on happily through the heart of Shakespeare's England; through Leamington and Kenilworth to Ashby de la Zouche. The two days that they spent at Merriden helped foster the better understanding that was developing between the former antagonists. To see Dominic, always in the background, apparently only idly interested in his brother's business dealings yet ever alert to support and further Oliver's wishes, ever watchful to prevent the possibility of over-fatigue, could not but give one a better notion of him, thought Chantal penitently. True, he was just as dictatorial as ever. But when his decisions were applied to someone other than herself, she could see that he was quite frequently right. The servants, too, obviously held him in respect and affection. There were enquiries after relatives, references to old-established jokes, reports on the progress of sons and daughters.

On the second day they rode together, she on Pegeen, he on a raking thoroughbred hunter of his father's. This was Quorn country, and they were happily absorbed in studying the great rolling fields, the banks and hedges, and in exchanging stories of gallant horses and sagacious hounds. They stopped at an isolated farmhouse round about noon and were warmly welcomed by the farmer's wife with offers of refreshment. They ate bacon sandwiches and wedges of green gooseberry pie. Dominic talked of crops and prices while Chantal admired the beautifully carved wooden cradle that stood on the hearth and talked gravely to its solemn-eyed occupant. She declined her hostess's offer of cowslip wine but accepted instead a mug of the home-brewed ale which had obviously won Dominic's approval.

'You always was a one for a bacon sandwich, wasn't you, milord?' said the good woman fondly, and was reluctant to let them go when, after suitable enquiries had been made as to her husband's health and a sovereign had been pressed into the baby's pink starfish fist, they bade her goodbye.

'She was one of the nursery maids when we were small,' said Dominic, as though feeling that this informal visit required some apology. 'Noll will be pleased that we managed to pay her a visit.' He put Chantal up and swung into the saddle himself. 'Makes a good brew of ale, too,' he grinned. 'Let us hope it does not prove too strong for you.'

Whether or no it was the influence of the ale, Chantal felt impelled to tease him a little. 'I am happy, milord,' she told him sweetly, 'that you can find *some* useful purpose for the female sex, even if it be only so humble a one as the brewing of ale. I had thought you considered us wholly superfluous.'

His mood met hers. 'Now what can have given you *that* idea?' he wondered innocently. 'No such thing, I promise you. I find women quite charming, if a little unreliable. The world would be a much more boring place without them. They are frequently ornamental. As for their usefulness' – his voice dropped to a confidential note – '*that* is a secret that has been known to my family for generations. I think it was during the French wars – or maybe after the Black Death – that the then Merriden noticed a lamentable shortage of lusty serfs to till the ancestral acres. Old men aplenty and women of all ages, but alas! No husbands for them, these poor wenches. He was a long-headed gentleman, this ancestor of mine. Perhaps he had a strong infusion of the de Montfort blood,' he put in provocatively. But she refused to rise to the jibe so he resumed solemnly, 'At the next manorial court he announced that in future he would forego the payment of merchet. The word was quickly spread. Within the year every cot in the vill had its tenant. New ones were building, thatches were mended, yardlands ploughed. And if some of the noble neighbours looked askance at the motley collection of old soldiers, runaway serfs and freedmen who had moved in, the village wiseacres were well pleased. They reckoned – and rightly, as it proved, that the newcomers would soon learn to walk meekly under the cat's foot. Equally pleased – or so results would seem to indicate – were the village maidens, now no longer condemned to go spinsters to the grave. Oh no! You cannot say that we Merridens set no value on women.'

Chantal had no idea what 'merchet' was, and no intention of betraying her ignorance. She said noncommittally, 'A provident gentleman indeed. One is compelled to admiration.'

The blue eyes lit to unholy mirth. She guessed that he had detected her subterfuge. What on earth *was* 'merchet'?

But he said only, with suspicious meekness, 'Would you like to let the horses out for a stretch?'

Six

'Oliver, what is the right of merchet?' demanded Chantal coming into the hall just before dinner. Oliver, who had been desultorily flicking over the pages of a book, looked up in rather natural surprise. What would the child be at next? She was a constant delight to him. He was watching the development of her relations with Dominic with the deepest interest. The more he saw them together the more convinced he was that they were well suited – if only they could be brought to acknowledge it. The thought of himself in the unlikely role of Eros brought a wry smile to his lips as he gave the required explanation.

'It was a marriage fine; in feudal times. When the daughter of a serf married, either her father or her husband had to pay a fee to the lord of the manor. It varied with the value of the girl,' he went on, warming to his subject, since he, too, found ancient customs fascinating. 'A skilled weaver or lacemaker was quite a valuable asset, and if she wished to marry away from the manor she and her children would become the property of a new manor lord.'

Chantal was silent, pulling thoughtfully at her lower lip. It seemed that this information did not quite fill her need for knowledge. Oliver said mischievously, 'I believe it was a valuable source of revenue when the parties most concerned had – er – anticipated the blessing of the Church.'

She blinked, and gazed at him wide-eyed, the light of comprehension dawning in her face. 'The wretch!' she said softly. 'No wonder he smiled!'

Oliver laughed outright at her expression. 'Do tell me,' he begged.

She twinkled back at him and did so. 'One can see why he found it so funny,' she admitted, 'but just let him say one more word about Simon de Montfort's methods. I wonder what was Eleanor's value in terms of merchet. Pretty high, would you not think?'

Dominic came in and found them laughing together but they refused to share the joke and Oliver turned the conversation to next day's journey. The stages now would be longer, he explained. 'We are passing into a harsh countryside, with little of beauty remaining for the traveller to enjoy. Though

I suppose there is much to admire if one considers the inventive genius that has gone to the making of the industries established there. For my part I can only be thankful that Providence has not condemned me to live in a town and heartily pity those who must do so. A hundred miles and more. Let us say three days before we are in open country and sweet air again. But be patient, for at the end of that time you shall see the finest scenery this side of the border.'

Dominic laughed. 'There spoke your Scottish blood,' he teased. 'We are mongrels, you must understand, Jan. But as soon as Oliver sniffs the border air he becomes all Scot. His very voice changes. By the end of the month he is practically unintelligible to a Southron ear. You will see. Indeed I entertain the gravest doubts about the wisdom of this prolonged stay in northern parts. It would not surprise me in the least if he were to don the white cockade and proclaim Papa as the rightful king of Scotland by virtue of some imagined tincture of Stuart blood.'

Oliver laughed too, but with a rueful quirk to the corners of his mouth which suggested that there might be some basis of truth for the absurd charge, and returned to the planning of next day's journey.

Chantal was quite sorry to leave Merriden. It was by no means so hideous as Dominic had given her to understand, and though it might be every bit as inconvenient as he had claimed, *she* was not required to manage it. She found it very comfortable indeed and was up betimes next morning to bid it farewell, strolling along the terraces, admiring the topiary work and passing into a very fine rose garden that was just coming into its full glory. The hound, Jester, joined her and insisted on prolonging the stroll until the chime of the stable clock sent Chantal hurrying back to the house, cheeks glowing, hair ruffled by her haste, to be scolded by Dominic for her tardiness.

'It was such a perfect morning,' she told him cheerfully. 'I went out to say goodbye to the house and Jester coaxed me down to the lake.' She accepted the plate of ham that he had carved for her and began her breakfast with good appetite. 'It's a lovely house,' she told them kindly. 'Not stiff and self-important like so many great houses, but friendly and welcoming. I wish I might be here in a week's time to see the roses.'

Both gentlemen looked gratified. 'We are really quite fond of it ourselves,' admitted Oliver. 'But just wait till you see Dorne.'

And he sounded quite unlike sedate mild-mannered Oliver in his eager anticipation.

The weather, which had favoured them so far, turned fickle. They passed from Derbyshire into Lancashire to the accompaniment of a shattering storm, and by the time they reached Manchester the rain had settled into a relentless downpour. Not until they reached Carlisle was there any real improvement, and all that Chantal saw of the fine scenery that Oliver had promised were the grim flanks of mountains whose crests were shrouded in mist and an occasional glimpse of steel-grey, rain-lashed water. Fortunately the three of them were now on such comfortable terms that the long hours of confinement passed more pleasantly than might have been expected. The brothers planned excursions to be made in the neighbourhood of Dorne. There was no wheeled traffic on the island itself they told her. Indeed it was so small that you could walk all round it in an afternoon. The stables and coach house were on the mainland.

Crossing the border was disappointing. The little river Sark was unimpressive and the countryside looked just the same. The two men teased her unmercifully when she voiced this opinion, but it was nothing to the roasting they gave her when she foolishly confessed to a naive interest in Gretna Green. Fortunately argument sprang up between them as to whether the marriages took place in the inn or in the smithy, so she was spared some of their mischievous suggestions as to the reason for her interest, and a timely shower prevented Dominic from fulfilling his threat of escorting her to inspect the premises for herself, partly to settle the argument but also in the hope that the blacksmith – or the innkeeper, if Oliver was in the right of it – would take them for an eloping couple.

'Think we are eloping – with all this cortege!' retorted Chantal scornfully, the toss of her head indicating the second carriage, the led horses and the bloodhound bitch lolloping happily along the muddy road. 'He is more likely to take us for an invading army than to mistake you for a prospective bridegroom.' Whereupon it was Oliver's turn to express pained surprise at her knowledge of the circumstances proper to an elopement. Between the two of them her cheeks were scarcely cool by the time they clattered into Dumfries.

Over supper that night they decided to

make a push to reach Dorne next day. Oliver was impatient to be home, and Oliver's wish was Dominic's law. So it was that they came down to Glenluce in the gloaming and Chantal saw the castle of Dorne outlined against the golden glory of the western sky and succumbed to its magic in that first breath.

No doubt it had been built on the tiny island for strategic reasons in the days of fierce family feuds. The sea made a natural barrier difficult to overcome in face of a determined defence. But those savage days were done, and the little dark castle floating so serenely between sea and sky was a castle out of a child's fairy tale. Chantal paid little heed to the business of transferring themselves and their belongings to the boats. She was vaguely aware that servants were bustling about between the carriages, the landing stage where she stood by Oliver's chair, and a group of buildings which must be the stables and the grooms' quarters that had been described to her. She heard the ring of Dominic's voice as he ordered the embarkation, but her gaze was held by the castle itself where now one or two golden lights glimmered, to be dimly reflected in the shadowed waters beneath the castle rock.

She was sleepy, drowsed with fresh air, for she had ridden a good deal of the way. Perhaps that accounted for her willing surrender to the spell of the place. Oliver, studying her air of bemusement with deep satisfaction, decided that this was just how the future Marchioness of Dorne *should* look, on first beholding the cradle of the family. When *his* day was done – and life was not so joyous a business that he wished it unduly prolonged – Dorne would be safe with Dominic and Chantal. Moreover, he reflected comfortably, he might now abandon his efforts to bring the two to terms. Dorne would do the business for him. Nothing could so endear Chantal to his difficult brother as this prompt capitulation. With a little sigh, half pleasure in his homecoming, half satisfaction with the prosperous way in which the future seemed to be shaping he drew Chantal's attention to the fact that the boats were now ready to shove off and only awaited their complement of passengers.

There was nothing to mar the girl's content. The sea was still as glass. The last streaks of crimson still lingered on the western horizon and the only sounds that broke the deep silence were the creak of the oars in the rowlocks and the gentle lapping of the water against the boat. Once they put up some birds who sounded indignant protest and promptly settled again a few yards away. Then they were drifting gently down to the castle landing stage, the short voyage over.

The path was lit by lanterns hung in the trees. So far as Chantal could see there seemed to be gardens bordering it, gardens filled with sweet scented plants and low-growing shrubs that cast grotesque shadows in the yellow lantern light. The path twisted and turned and gradually climbed, making the most of the island's limited area, so that it took them some time to reach the sturdy oaken door that stood welcomingly open. Though it was mid-June a fire glowed cheerfully on the wide stone hearth of the hall, where Murdoch, the steward of Dorne, was waiting to greet them and to enquire their wishes as to refreshment. Lady Celia, he said, had not really expected them until next day and had dined at her usual hour, but a meal could be served to them at once if they desired it.

'We dined in Newton Stewart,' Oliver told him. 'And we are all tired. An early night, I think, once we have greeted Aunt Celia.'

Dominic nodded. 'A bowl of negus in the gun room,' he suggested. And then to Chantal, 'Would you like that? It is really very harmless.'

But Chantal declined; saying that she would rather go straight to bed and would prefer hot milk. Hilda nodded austere approval and went off to unpack her mistress's night-rail and see that her bed was nicely warmed. It might be high summer, but the sea air was cool and there was nothing like a warm bed to induce sound sleep.

They would find Lady Celia in the Tower room, said Murdoch, so Dominic and Chantal climbed the winding stone stair to this apartment while the steward pushed Oliver's chair into the gunroom. It was like stepping back into a historic past, thought Chantal, as her fingers touched the rough-hewn stone walls that had stood firm for centuries. She noted narrow lancet windows and steps worn away by the tread of countless feet, and looked forward eagerly to days of leisurely exploration.

The Tower room was roughly circular, and its stone walls, cavernous hearth and heavy furniture might have come straight from the pages of a mediaeval romance. But the windows had been modernised. The arrow slits of Chantal's imagining had given place to large casements, one of which stood open to admit the sound of the sea. Lady Celia was sitting at a table heaped with papers peering at a small volume bound in rusty vellum, holding it close under the lamp in an attempt to decipher the faded writing. Chantal discovered later that it was the household book of a long-dead chatelaine of Dorne. Lady Celia had embarked on the formidable task of writing a family history and, immersed in the fascinating pages that recorded her predecessor's struggles with dirt, sickness, the difficulty of obtaining supplies of fresh food and the best ways of preserving such meat and fish as were readily obtainable, had quite forgotten the impending arrival of two living Merridens and their guest.

She was a slight little creature looking scarcely old enough to be Dominic's aunt. She had the dominant Merriden nose but her eyes were still beautiful, shaped and set like Dominic's, but the vivid blue of his deepened, in Celia's, to shadowed violet.

She put down her book and came forward swiftly, standing on tiptoe to kiss her tall nephew's cheek. 'Dear boy,' she said happily. 'So nice to have you here for the whole summer; and Oliver, too. Murdoch *did* remind me, but the time must have slipped away. I had meant to be in the hall to greet you. Pray forgive me. And this is little Jan.' She put out a slim hand and pressed Chantal's kindly. 'My good-sister tells me that you have been sadly pulled down by the anxieties that you have suffered. Poor child! We shall soon set that to rights, here at Dorne. The boys will look after you and keep you entertained, but don't let them tease you to attempt anything that is beyond your strength.' She surveyed the girl more critically and added, with a slightly puzzled air, 'Though I must say you look to me to be in high bloom.'

'The journey has done much to restore Jan to her usual self,' interposed Dominic smoothly. 'We took things very easily so that we should not overtire her. But Mama is insistent that she live secluded for a while and Dorne seemed to be the very place. No morning callers here, and no persistent suitors either. She may be at peace and do just as she likes.'

Lady Celia murmured sympathetic agreement and then, on a more bracing note declared, 'If you are to be here for the whole summer, you must sit for me. It need not interfere with your pleasuring – there are bound to be plenty of wet days – and it will be delightful to have a new subject. Do say yes.'

Naturally Chantal said that she would be only too happy to be of use to her hostess. Lady Celia patted her kindly, told her that she must be sure to take breakfast in bed until she felt stronger, added vaguely, 'So like dear Fiona Macdonald,' and said that she must go and greet her other nephew. She then flitted off, leaving Dominic shaking with laughter and Chantal slightly dazed.

'Who is Fiona Macdonald?' she asked him, puzzled.

'A girl from the islands who married a Merriden back in 1715,' he told her, smiling. 'There is a portrait of her in the music room. And yes, there is a likeness. Trust Aunt Celia to notice it right away. Something about the modelling of the brows and temples and the shape of your mouth.' He chuckled. 'By all accounts *she* had the devil's own temper, too,' he said provocatively.

But Chantal declined the challenge and said demurely that she was rather tired and would be grateful if he would summon one of the maids to show her to her room. He preferred, however, to perform this service himself, explaining that, knowing her love of antiquities, he had suggested that she be given one of the upper tower rooms.

'Though I fear your maid will not share your enthusiasm,' he warned her. 'Oliver and I are housed in the other tower. We always preferred those rooms when we were children and many's the phantom fleet we've espied from our beleaguered fortress. Alas for the onset of old age that such imaginings have lost their charm! And here we are.' He held open the door for her. 'And here is Hilda. I leave you in good hands. Sleep well. You will have the sea to sing your lullaby.'

'I know naught of sea lullabies,' said Hilda practically as the door closed behind him, 'but it's a Sabbath day's journey to bring you a can of hot water, miss. Though I will say there's plenty of willing hands to help a body. And maybe it's as well for you and me to be together in this tower with the two gentlemen in the other and her ladyship in between. More proper that way. And it's thankful I am to find I can understand the way they talk – mostly, any way, though there's one or two words that are strange to me. You'd scarcely know you was in a foreign country, would you?' she ended in a burst of confidence.

Further investigation revealed that Hilda had never before travelled north of Trent. Chantal realised that it had required quite a degree of courage to agree to such an adventure.

'But I likes it pretty well,' the girl told her, encouraged by the friendly interest. 'Let me do those buttons, miss. The bath water's going cold and it's stiff and sore you'll be tomorrow after all that riding unless you takes your bath good and hot.'

Chantal was indeed tired – too sleepy to devote much attention to the delightful room that had been allotted her except to decide sleepily that with the walls hung with tapestries and a screen to keep out any wandering draughts it was really very cosy. She had not even finished the glass of hot milk that Hilda brought before sleep claimed her. The abigail, tiptoeing about the room as she hung out the last of the travel-creased garments, put out the candles and stole away well satisfied.

Seven

The weeks that followed were the happiest that Chantal had ever known. The country way of life suited her to a nicety. Far from breakfasting in bed, she and Dominic rode together very early each fine day. That meant crossing to the mainland of course, but there was a neat little dinghy that made light work of that. Sometimes they rode along the coastal track that ran south towards the headland, sometimes on the sands themselves, Dominic warning that it was dangerous to ride, or, indeed, to walk on the sands to the north and west of the bay as there were treacherous quicksands in that area, and emphasising the warning with grim tales of shipwreck.

They would go back ravenously hungry to consume an enormous breakfast in company with Oliver and make plans for the day. They would go sailing or swimming or fishing. Chantal took but a modest part in the fishing expeditions. It seemed only fair to make *some* effort after the pains they had taken over her instruction, but when, with much urgent advice and a little assistance she actually caught a small sea trout she could only regret the poor thing's demise. It was scarcely big enough to eat, and she could see little satisfaction in killing just for the fun of the thing.

A statement to this effect provoked fierce argument, the men urging the delights of pitting one's wits and skill against a wary adversary, Dominic administering a clincher by asking why she went hunting if that was how she felt.

'For the excitement,' she admitted honestly. 'And because my father was pleased and proud if I could keep up with him. I'm afraid I never thought about the fox. I just loved the speed and the feel of a good horse under me. Any way, foxes are vermin,' she added defensively, realising that her candour was playing into their hands. 'This poor thing was doing no harm.' She nudged the trout gingerly with her toe.

'You should enquire the opinion of the smaller marine creatures about that,' suggested Oliver with an amused twinkle.

She raised her brows enquiringly.

'He eats them, you know. Not only insects and worms, but little fish and even fish eggs.

I daresay every mama fish for miles around is calling down blessings on your head for so gallantly removing this menace to her young.'

Chantal looked aggrievedly at her trophy. He had only helped Oliver to demolish her argument. And Dominic had pulled out a sketching block and a stick of charcoal and with swift economical strokes was depicting a row of assorted fish standing on their tails, fins upraised in praise or supplication, all addressing themselves to a Chantal who had mysteriously acquired a mermaid's tail. She had to laugh at the comical caricature, though she was firm in her refusal to fish again.

Sometimes they went further afield, foregoing the morning ride and setting out early to visit some ancient abbey or castle – none, vowed Chantal loyally, one half so lovely as Dorne – or the bustling little port of Stranraer with its magnificent views over Loch Ryan towards Arran and Kintyre. The days fled all too swiftly. So did the long leisurely evenings when it was never really dark. They would open the long windows of the music room and the scent of the sea would drift in to them, mingled with the sweetness of stocks and roses and mignonette, as they talked over the day's events, or argued, as they had done about hunting and fishing, or lit the candles and made music together if the mood so took them.

When it was really too hot to venture out even on the water, they lazed in the coolness of the garden. Generations of Merridens had given their care to the making of that garden. Soil had been brought from the mainland to supplement the light sandy covering bestowed by nature. There was one garden that was all blue and silver, where sea lavender and sea holly grew in the shelter of a buckthorn hedge and hydrangeas queened it proudly. There were hedges ablaze with the gold of hypericum, or Rose of Sharon, its prettier name which Chantal preferred. The turf was green and springy, gemmed with rosy flowers of thrift; the sea so smooth it might have been a lake, save for the tiny ripples that betrayed the incoming tide. Somehow argument arose about the reading matter appropriate to the female intellect, but it was too hot to argue properly. Chantal dropped down on the grass by Oliver's chair and yielded to the languor of the still afternoon. Dominic, having wedged the chair securely, announced that he must go back to the house.

'Letters to write,' he groaned, 'that must catch tomorrow's mail. Deal faithfully with this wayward chit, won't you, Noll? Next we shall have her demanding the works of Mary Godwin.'

He strolled off. As they watched him go, the moment seemed to Chantal opportune to satisfy a growing curiosity.

'It's a very odd circumstance,' she began. 'When we were at Claverton, *you* were forever engaged in business and letter writing. Your brother and I almost came to cuffs because I took him to task for leaving all the work to you. Here at Dorne it is the other way about. *You* are the one who idles in the garden while he is for ever excusing himself on the plea of letters to write.'

There was a glint in Oliver's eyes. This was interesting. For a girl of Chantal's breeding to express such a degree of concern over his brother's affairs was surely significant. He *could* have told her that some of the time that Nick spent shut away in his room was devoted to painting a portrait of herself. He did not do so. Instead he said carelessly, 'Oh – I daresay you have realised by now that Nick is by no means the idler he would have you believe. He is concerned in a great many affairs and gets through a vast amount of business in his lazy-seeming way.'

With that she had to be content. It did not prevent her from spending a good deal of time in speculation as to the nature of the business in which his lordship was concerned.

Oliver, too, was indulging in a certain amount of speculation. From what he had heard, the portrait that his brother was painting was unusual to say the least of it. He would have given a handsome sum for a glimpse of it.

He had come by his knowledge innocently enough. He had salvaged the charcoal sketch of Chantal and the fish and directed his man to pin it up on the wall because it amused him. Some days later he had sent Bateson up to Dominic's room with a letter which had been accidentally included with his own mail. On his return the valet had volunteered the information that his lordship was engaged on an enlarged version of the sketch in oils.

'Only it don't look the same,' he had said in a perplexed sort of way. But when pressed he could only say that the *fish* looked different – 'not comical, like those' – and that he had not seen very much because milord had swiftly stepped between him and the painting. The situation, decided Oliver, was developing nicely.

Dominic was less satisfied with the course of events. If he had dreamed that his sentiments towards Chantal could undergo such a change, he would never have agreed that she should take refuge at Dorne. To be sure he had developed quite a liking for the girl on the journey north. Once or twice he had even found himself reflecting that it might have been rather pleasant to have a young sister to tease and to cosset.

It was only since their arrival at Dorne that warmer feelings had sprung to life. Her complete capitulation to the charm of the place had pleased him greatly. He found himself studying her face as he showed her some corner of his home beloved since childhood; even asking her opinion of projected innovations. At first this had been all. But constant propinquity and an unconventional degree of freedom had wrought an insidious spell. Of late he had found himself obliged to keep the lady at a distance. One could resist the temptation to kiss the nape of her neck where the soft hair curled in little feathery tendrils as she stooped to examine some sea creature or strange flower, but her mouth, with its full upper lip and its unconscious pathos in repose, tempted him maddeningly. Dominic was no monk. He had enjoyed occasional light affairs with a variety of young ladies who understood perfectly well what they were about, but never before had he felt any desire for a more serious attachment.

Chantal was no lady of easy virtue to whom he could offer a carte blanche. This time desire must be kept within bounds. Not only was she a guest in his home but she also had a claim on his protective chivalry. And it did not make matters easier that she treated him with a warm friendliness that was the mark of her innocence. When she had stretched up, laughing, to remove a large furry caterpillar that was painstakingly ascending his shoulder, he had been hard put to it to refrain from catching her in his arms and kissing that inviting mouth. Chantal had been quite unaware, concerned only for the caterpillar, and had run off with it cradled in her palm in search of Oliver who would undoubtedly be able to name its species and describe its life cycle.

He had hoped, by painting her portrait, to ease a little of his pent-up restlessness, but in this he had lamentably failed. Some last upsurge of the bitterness that he had nourished for so many years had caused him to paint a Chantal who wore a cold, inscrutable half-smile as she gazed through her mirror at the adoring fish. Small wonder that poor Bateson, after one brief glimpse, had said that the fish looked different. They had been given the faces of men. Dominic had enjoyed painting those fish. Several notorious men-of-the-town might have found them cause sufficient for libel action, for each face depicted a different form of desire, from the sheep-eyed yearning of a loose-lipped weakling to the rampant lust of a middle-aged rake.

He stood back to study the finished effect. It was vile. Exhibited at Somerset House it would bring him overnight notoriety. Society would be all agog to identify the 'fish'. And Chantal – confiding, innocent Chantal – would be smeared by every kind of foul insinuation. It would be a kind of rape, he thought furiously, and quite without justification, for the expression of cynical calculation on the painted face was a lie. Chantal had never looked so in her life. Could not look so. Mistakes she might have made – been guilty of any number of youthful follies, but in that moment he knew he would stake his life on her truth and her loyalty.

He gave the picture one last long look and then, very deliberately, picked up the knife that he used for scraping his palette and slashed it across and across until it was reduced to unrecognisable shreds. Satisfied at last, he stretched, yawned and shook himself as one awaking from some evil dream and began, with the utmost care, to prepare another canvas. A little smile curved his mouth as he worked. How should he paint her, his rebel maid? Sailing the skiff, as she loved to do, or riding Pegeen? Frolicking with Jester, perhaps. No hurry to decide. He could count on two more months at least unless winter set in uncommonly early. That should be sufficient, not only for painting a portrait but also to woo a girl as independent and virginal as Diana's self. It might not be easy. After her experience with her unpleasant cousin she would naturally be wary.

No thought of the possible activities of that gentleman disturbed his happy frame of mind. So light-hearted and relaxed was he over dinner that they were all affected by his mood. When Aunt Celia asked, interpreting his gaiety by her own feelings, if his painting had gone well, his answer was prompt.

'At least it has gone. And a deal of spite and ugliness with it.' He smiled at their puzzled faces. 'I have been trying my hand at a rather fanciful allegory,' he explained. 'In the process a good deal of poison was transferred to the canvas, and I confess to feeling the better for having voided it. I have destroyed the unpleasant result and mean to start again. If you will permit me, Jan, I would like to attempt a portrait of you. See if I can beat Aunt Celia at her own game,' he teased that lady, who was already engaged on a portrait of Chantal dressed in a charming costume of early Georgian times that might well have been worn by Fiona Macdonald herself.

Chantal coloured delightfully at the implied compliment but demurred, saying that to be sitting for two artists would take up a great deal of time, and with the weather so fine it seemed a pity to spend so long indoors.

'Oh, but I have nearly done,' protested Lady Celia helpfully, 'and I can very well work on the costume and background without you.'

So Chantal, who had instinctively sought to evade an assignment that would mean long periods alone with Dominic, was compelled to agree. She did not know how clearly her expression mirrored her inward doubts and so was considerably comforted when he said meditatively that he rather thought he should paint her in an outdoor setting and that Oliver could make himself useful by entertaining the sitter.

He was careful, too, to avoid Chantal's eyes when he sang for them that night. Lady Celia had offered to play his accompaniments so that it would have been easy to sing *at* the girl, but though he might be deep in love he had sufficient good sense remaining to realise that such particularity could only embarrass her. So he sang 'Drink to me only' and 'The Bonnie Earl o' Moray' in his smooth beguiling baritone, and only when he came to the last line of 'There is a lady sweet and kind' did he permit his glance to rest briefly on the girl's rapt, upturned face. For a long moment blue eyes, at last unguarded, looked steadily into startled grey ones. Some wordless message passed between them. Chantal's hands flew to her lips, a betraying gesture which she hurriedly covered by making pretence of polite applause. Her heart was racing as though she had been running. Across the space that divided them she had *felt* the kiss that he would have pressed on her mouth. Through her confusion she heard Oliver placidly remark that his brother was in good voice. Lady Celia, fingers idling over the keys, presently strayed into a dance tune, an old Scottish air in waltz rhythm, and some imp of mischief prompted Oliver to suggest, with a grandfatherly air, that the young folk dance. Since Lady Celia immediately supported the notion, Chantal submitted with the best grace she could muster. In the general way she loved dancing, but to be taken in Dominic's arms at that precise moment was an ordeal that demanded all her self control.

He contented himself with two or three circuits of the limited space at their disposal, thanked his partner gravely for the pleasure of the dance and asked if she would be willing to play a measure so that he could dance with Aunt Celia.

Nothing could have served better. Chantal promptly decided that she had refined too much on that oddly intimate exchange of glances. Thankfully she played the delicate minuet that Lady Celia requested; was even sufficiently recovered to watch over her shoulder the charming picture that the dancers made as they performed the old fashioned measure with grave precision. But when Dominic suggested that she dance with him again, she begged off, saying that she was really too sleepy to mind her steps.

He did not press the request. He was pretty well pleased with his progress but he knew it behoved him to tread warily. When the tea tray was brought in he carried her cup to her but did not seek to engage her in conversation. Oliver mentioned idly that Murdoch had reported tinklers camping in the glen and the men discussed the plague of petty pilfering and the depredations on the local poultry population that would probably follow. Gentle Lady Celia said she thought tinklers were often blamed for sins they did not commit. Every poacher for miles around would take advantage of their presence to step up his own activities.

'And they are so picturesque,' she told Chantal, as though this was excuse sufficient for lack of moral principle. 'You must be sure and pay a visit to the encampment.'

'Yes, indeed,' agreed Oliver, at his most mischievous. 'Get one of the old dames to tell your fortune. Cross her palm with silver and she'll promise you a fine handsome husband.'

'But don't cuddle the babies, attractive as

they are, or we shall have Hilda declaring that your dress must be burned,' advised Dominic more soberly. For once he felt that Oliver's teasing was ill-timed. Of course he could not know of the revelation that had been vouchsafed to his brother and so must be forgiven. The subject of fortune telling was allowed to drop. Dominic turned to ask Lady Celia if she had found the silk she wanted for the new curtains, so Chantal must run up to the Tower room and bring down the snippets that the mercer had sent and they all proceeded to air their views without reaching any definite conclusion. Since Lady Celia would undoubtedly make her own choice in the end, this was of small consequence.

There was no opportunity for outdoor portrait painting during the next few days for they brought wind and rain that battered the roses and lashed the shallow waters of the bay into dramatic fury. Lady Celia, mildly triumphant, completed *her* portrait of her young guest, a charming if slightly sentimental representation of a maiden leaning from her casement to catch the first glimpse of a lover returning from the wars. The younger members of the party beguiled the time according to temperament and inclination. Dominic's inclination seemed to lead him surprisingly often into Chantal's vicinity.

After three days of confinement their usual pastimes began to pall. It was Oliver who suggested hide and seek, with the hound, Jester, as the seeker. He engaged himself to keep her in leash beside his chair while the others concealed themselves – or laid a trail for her, as her master preferred to phrase it – and to loose her at an agreed time, first permitting her to snuff some article that the 'fugitives' had handled. On the first attempt Chantal was a little shy and stiff, feeling that she was really too old for such childish games. But Dominic had fortunately chosen a refuge in one of the attics and they were able to peer over the stair head and watch their pursuer as she sniffed out their tracks with what seemed to the girl uncanny accuracy until she was near enough to identify them by sight.

They experimented. Chantal's kerchief and gloves, Dominic's whip and one of his shoes were used in turn. The hound justified her master's pride in her abilities. At the end of half an hour a breathless laughing Chantal was scampering up stairs and along corridors, flushed with exercise and a little untidy as to hair, catching willingly at Dominic's hand as it was extended to help her up a steep spiral stair or to steer her along a dark passage way, with never a thought for the dignity demanded of a damsel of twenty years.

The game came to an end eventually because Dominic said that it would be unfair to cross their own earlier tracks. A good hound would follow a trail up to forty eight hours old and there was a limit to the number of different routes that they could use.

'But we could do this out of doors when the weather mends,' suggested Chantal eagerly. And Dominic assented willingly and was thankful that he had not succumbed to the temptation to snatch a kiss in those dark corridors. He did not think she was ready, yet, for kisses, but he was well pleased with his morning's work.

The weather improved next day, but since Lady Celia had asked Chantal to go with her to the mercer's in Newton Stewart there was no opportunity of trying Jester's powers over a wider terrain.

'Though we should certainly do so at the first opportunity,' offered Oliver solemnly. 'What a relief to all our minds to know that, should we chance to mislay you in some remote corner of this vast estate, we have an infallible means of tracking you down!' And Chantal giggled at his absurdity and went to put on her hat.

The ladies did not hurry themselves. Having settled the important business of ordering the silk for the new curtains they embarked on a leisurely shopping saunter. It was early evening when they came back to Glenluce, pleasantly tired with their wanderings and, Chantal realised, with a warm sense of home-coming. She was looking forward to relating the small events of the day over dinner and to hearing what Oliver and Dominic had been doing during their absence. As the carriage turned into their own lane Lady Celia exclaimed with interest, 'See, my dear! That must be one of the tinklers that Murdoch spoke of. But what a strange looking fellow! Not at all the usual type. They are gypsies really, you know. Or Egyptians, as some of the older ones claim – members of a wandering tribe from some Eastern land. Many of them are extremely handsome in youth. I have never seen one look surly and hang-dog like that fellow. Did you see how he slunk into the hedge as though to escape our notice?'

Chantal had not seen the man very clearly from her side of the carriage, but once her attention had been drawn to him she was struck by a sense of familiarity. Somewhere she had seen him before. Perhaps he, too, had been in Newton Stewart. They might well have passed him in the street. At which point the carriage drew up at the landing stage and she forgot all about him.

The halcyon weather returned and they were able to take up their outdoor pursuits again. Jester displayed her tracking abilities to Chantal's delight and admiration and Dominic made a start on her portrait. His stern self restraint was now paying handsome dividends. Chantal was well aware that he was paying her the most distinguishing attention. He did not fuss over it – but whatever she needed for her comfort or her entertainment was always to hand. He did not treat her as some, poor feeble creature incapable of athletic effort but he was careful that she was not overtired or allowed to stray into danger. Chantal was no fool. She had gone through a London season and she knew very well how a man behaved when he wished to indulge in a pleasant flirtation. This was something different again. Incredible as it seemed, she could only believe that he was serious.

To herself she admitted that she liked him more than a little; even that it might be very enjoyable to feel that imagined kiss actually pressed upon her mouth. But love – and marriage – were serious matters. They were for life. Did she want to surrender herself and her life into his keeping? His seeming idleness still troubled her. And so did his arrogance. There was no doubt that he would be the master of his household. He would cherish his wife, but he would expect her to be submissive and obedient. Chantal was not at all sure that she wanted to be either. There were moments, as she considered her own situation, when she felt that she would thankfully barter her freedom for a claim on Dominic's protection. And that was a fine reason for marrying a man she thought scornfully, despising her own cowardice. If she could not truly love him without reckoning the advantages he could give her, then he was better without her.

Eight

She had not meant to eavesdrop. She had been sunning herself on the terrace outside the open windows of the music room when Dominic had brought her a letter from her London attorney which had been sent under cover to him. So he must have been aware of her presence. Indeed she had not heard the first part of the conversation between the brothers since she had been engaged in scanning the brief content of Mr. Parker's letter. It said little of moment. The authorities had not, so far, met with any success in their efforts to apprehend Mr. Dickensen's assailants. He trusted that she was enjoying her stay in the north and he enclosed a draft on a Scottish bank which his lordship would cash for her.

She folded the draft and the letter together – and heard Dominic say, 'No. I'm afraid I'll have to go myself. A damned nuisance, particularly just now. But there *have* been impostors, and I prefer to make my own investigations. It's a remarkably smooth letter – too smooth by half – something a trifle smoky about it.'

Oliver must have been sitting with his back to her, for though she could hear the murmur of his voice she did not catch the words. There was an answering chuckle from Dominic. He said, 'Well, naturally. I would have preferred to have something settled first. But it's no good sending Murdoch. When it comes to estate business or to buying stock he's as shrewd as he can hold together, but being honest himself he's inclined to take other men at face value. There's nothing for it but to go myself. I need not be away above one night if all goes well. The place is on the outskirts of Ayr, and if I take Rusty over the first stage I should manage it in the day.'

Another murmur from Oliver. Then, 'No. Not Pegeen. I'll leave her for Chantal – but you'll see she takes a groom with her, won't you? I don't really care to have her going over to the mainland while I'm not at hand to see she comes to no harm. She's safe enough here, but I don't trust that objectionable cousin of hers. He's kept too quiet for my liking. If she was promised to me I'd not allow her to leave the island during my absence, but she's never been accustomed to the curb and I daren't risk a direct order.'

Chantal heard Oliver's laugh. She would dearly have loved to vent her indignation on the conniving wretches but it had just been born in upon her that she had been listening, however innocently, to a conversation not intended for her ears. She must swallow her wrath and maintain a demurely smiling front however difficult the task. Unpractised in dissimulation and still seething over the remark about the curb, she made no attempt to slip away unperceived. Indeed she was still preoccupied with sorting out the snatches of conversation that she had heard. She was not particularly interested in Dominic's business trip, but she would dearly have liked to know what it was that he had wanted to see settled before he left. Herself, perhaps? How right she had been to think him too domineering to make a satisfactory husband! So he would forbid her to leave the island, would he? They would see about that!

Simmering down slightly after an energetic hour with Jester on the beach, she was prepared to admit that at least his thoughts had been for her safety and her pleasure. He was even prepared to give up his beloved

Pegeen for her use, and that when he was setting out on a long journey where the mare would have been invaluable. But she still could not forgive that remark about the curb!

Consequently she deliberately delayed her return to the house until she knew that he must have left and was decidedly cool to Oliver over lunch. Oliver, who had observed her offended departure from the terrace and guessed that she had heard remarks not intended for her ears, did not blame her. Any woman of spirit would have resented them, he thought, but added a mental rider that only a woman of spirit would do for Dominic. If he married that gentle docile creature of his brother's earlier imaginings he would soon reduce her to nonentity, and then she would bore him. If *this* pair eventually made a match of it, Oliver could foresee some royal battles, but he thought that in general they would deal extremely together and would be very happy.

He said pleasantly, 'I'm afraid you will have to make do with my society for a day or two. Nick is gone to Ayr on business. He has left Pegeen for your use, and begs that you will not ride out without a groom while he is away.'

The lady put her little nose in the air at this expurgated version of Dominic's remarks. How delightful it was to hear that his lordship 'begged'! With crushing civility she said that she would not dream of doing anything that would displease Lady Celia.

Oliver hid his amusement. He enquired politely what she would like to do in the afternoon, but on hearing that she meant to spend it lazily, reading one of the sadly neglected novels that she had brought with her, felt that it was safe to leave her to her own devices. He understood her feelings pretty well and guessed that she would love to make some gesture of defiance that would put Dominic in his place, but he also knew that she would not lie about her intentions.

In fact the day passed very peacefully indeed, save that Chantal was a little dismayed to discover how often her thoughts strayed towards the absentee. Nor could she convince herself that it was because she was displeased with him. Now that her quick temper had had time to cool, she allowed that his *sentiments* had been praiseworthy even if his expression of them was regrettably crude. It was not long before she sought solace for this new kind of loneliness by asking Oliver about the journey to Ayr. How long would it take? How many times must one change horses? Would milord stay at an inn or had he friends in the town?

Oliver answered her questions as though such curiosity was perfectly understandable and went on, in the most obliging fashion, to talk of his brother, expressing the pleasure it gave him to see Dominic so well entertained and so content with quiet Dorne. 'For he is a restless, energetic creature, you know, and frequently drives himself too hard.'

Chantal stared at him in some surprise. He returned the look with bland serenity. The urge to discover more – perhaps to set at rest her doubts about his lordship's way of life – was irresistible.

'That is the second time that you have referred to your brother's energetic disposition,' she told him frankly, 'and for the life of me I cannot see why. Save for the fact that he both writes and receives a great many letters, he appears to me to spend his life wholly in the pursuit of pleasure. Are you not, perhaps, unduly prejudiced in his favour?'

It was Oliver's turn to stare. And for once there was a very stern expression on his pleasant face. 'At the moment,' he said, speaking temperately with an obvious effort, 'my brother is on holiday after months of arduous work. Can you not see the difficulties of his position? If I had been a whole man, he would have been free to follow his own inclination, and I think there is small doubt that he would have carved out a distinguished career for himself in the world of politics. As it is, he lends me his strength and stands always in my shadow, yet still finds time and energy to work for those causes in which he profoundly believes. For years he has been an ardent supporter of the campaign for emancipation. With that battle won, and poor Wilberforce's death, he has turned his attention to the sufferings of the factory and mine workers in our own land. You saw something of the places in which the poor creatures live on our journey north. Were you aware that not only men but women and little children work as much as twelve or fifteen hours a day in the most appalling conditions? That women work underground, dragging trucks like beasts of burden? Young Ashley Cooper has dedicated himself to the task of ending these shameful practices, and my brother has pledged his support. If that is not sufficient to satisfy your zeal for action, he also devotes most of his personal fortune to the maintenance of a home for men who have been crippled or blinded in their country's service. It should not tax your powers of understanding too far to guess the reason for this particular form of benevolence. He himself supervises the admission of deserving candidates and appoints the officers whose task is to make life as comfortable as possible for the poor wretches – such a task as he himself performs for me. He can never give himself wholly to a political career because he will not desert me. Do you think it is easy for a man of Dominic's stamp that he must always stand aside – always come second?'

So stern a reprimand from the usually tolerant Oliver was shattering. Chantal whitened a little and her lips quivered. But there was a glow in her eyes that had nothing to do with contrition. When he added suddenly, 'Do you still think me absurdly prejudiced?' she held up her head and met his gaze squarely.

'No. But had you given me even a hint of some of these activities when first we spoke on this head, I might have been spared a crushing set-down. You may say that your brother's affairs are none of my business, and so far as his philanthropies are concerned I would hold you justified. But you could have given me some hint of his political activities instead of allowing me to go on thinking him an indolent do-nothing.'

Oliver grinned. How very right he had been in his estimate of the lady's character! Interesting, too – and very satisfactory – to discover that only a man of action could claim her whole-hearted allegiance, since he had reason to believe that her love had been won long since.

'A hit,' he acknowledged, 'a palpable hit. But I *did* tell you that he was not so idle as he showed and got through a deal of work without undue fuss.'

'I set that down to your natural loyalty,' she confessed. 'He never speaks of serious matters. On the one or two occasions when we have spoken of the responsibilities that go with high rank, he has turned the whole thing into a joke. How could I be expected to guess that he is deeply concerned for the welfare of his fellow men?'

'Well – he showed a certain amount of concern for yours,' suggested Oliver, smiling, 'And that despite his absurd prejudice against your sex – a prejudice, by the way, which he seems at last to have conquered.'

She coloured a little at that but made no reply. 'As for his flippancy, I fear a good deal of that, too, must be laid at your door. He said that you had been robbed of a year of your youth and that he wanted your stay at Dorne to be as carefree and lighthearted as we could make it. But to speak truth, that same carefree holiday has done *him* a great deal of good, too, so we won't splinter lances on that head. Shall we cry pax, and agree that he is an infuriating wretch, who may mean well but whose clumsy efforts in no way match his intentions?'

Chantal laughed and put out an impulsive hand. Oliver shook it firmly and their brief discord was over.

The evening was still very warm. Lady Celia, who had spent all day shut up in her room engrossed in an attempt to trace an obscure collateral branch of the family, came down to bid them good night and to announce that she meant to retire early, as poring over the crabbed and faded handwriting of the various documents had given her a headache. The two on the terrace sat on, content in each other's company, each busy with thoughts that were not yet for sharing. Presently Oliver roused himself to suggest a day-long sailing picnic for the morrow if the weather held good and they wrangled amicably about the best venue for such an expedition, though Oliver seemed to be more concerned with studying the view of the mainland and the lane that ran down to the landing stage. From time to time he would shade his eyes with his hand and peer into the distance. Chantal looked too, but she could see nothing out of the ordinary. When, for the fourth or fifth time he turned his head and failed to answer some casual question, she asked him frankly if he was expecting a visitor.

He shook his head and apologised for his abstraction.

'No. But I was hoping that Murdoch would be returned by now. A message was brought to him just after Nick left to say that his brother had met with an accident.'

He went on to explain that David – the brother – had broken a leg and perhaps suffered some head injury as well. To make matters worse, Margaret, David's wife, was expecting a child and was near her time. Murdoch had not wanted to desert his post while 'the young master' was away, but he was naturally very anxious about his relations and Oliver had finally persuaded him to ride over to Wigtown, where his brother worked as bailiff on a large estate, and find out what was happening, since the lad who had brought the message had been unable to give them any further details.

'It's not so very far, cross country on a good horse. I'd expected him back by now. I fear he has found matters more serious than we had hoped.'

They sat on in silence, both of them straining their eyes towards the lane as though the very intensity of their gaze could summon up the familiar figure of the steward. Suddenly Oliver gave a sharp exclamation.

'Look! Over there – to the right of the coach house. Can you see a glow? Yes, and flames too. Something's afire. And it's growing.'

Chantal sprang to her feet to get a better view. The glow was spreading rapidly, and now they could make out one or two black figures outlined against the flames. The grooms, no doubt, trying to extinguish the blaze and, so far as the onlookers could make out, with small success. For a minute or two they watched, horror stricken. Then Chantal cried out on a little whimper of mingled fear and pity, 'Oliver! The horses. Pegeen! I don't think they've got them out.

We must have seen them if they were in the paddock.'

As Oliver's shocked exclamation confirmed her fear, she said sharply, 'I'm going across. We can't just sit here and watch them burn to death. Though what the grooms are about – it should have been their first thought. Don't worry about me. I promise to be sensible and not take foolish risks, but you must see that I have to go.'

'And I'm coming with you,' said Oliver. 'I can't be any help to you in getting the horses out, but I can row you across to the other side in half the time that you could do it yourself. Push me down to the beach – and hurry. Thank God the boat was just pulled up on the sand. Otherwise we'd never have made it in time.'

Even so it took all Chantal's strength to drag the boat down to the water's edge and steady it while Oliver, with a desperate effort, managed somehow to lever himself up on his arms and more or less fall into it. But once launched he easily made good his promise. From constant use his arms and shoulders were unusually strong, and the boat shot across the bay at racing speed.

Chantal sprang out as it nosed the landing stage. Oliver could do no more to help her.

Without his wheel chair he was virtually a prisoner in the boat. He called a final warning as she ran for the stables. Something about covering the horses' eyes. She remembered that from some tale she had read. If you blindfolded them, you could sometimes manage to lead a terrified animal to safety.

It was no more than two hundred yards to the threatened building, but on the loose sandy surface of the path it felt like a mile. As she struggled breathlessly up the slope there was time to realise thankfully that the fire posed no immediate threat to the stable. Thanks to the direction of the wind it was progressing more swiftly towards the coach house and the grooms' quarters that stood beyond it, but it was also steadily eating back towards the stable block. Perhaps the threat to their homes and belongings accounted for the absence of the grooms, but it was inexcusable that they should not first have seen to the safety of their charges. She tugged open the heavy door, trying to control her breathing, to remember that now she must move steadily and calmly. Hasty movements, nervous hands, would only add to the terror of animals already frightened by the smell of smoke and the unusual noises outside. She was thankful that Dominic had taken Rusty, a powerful beast with a fine turn of speed but temperamental and difficult to handle. Gentle Pegeen responded at once to the familiar voice and allowed herself to be led out into the paddock with no more than a hand grasping her mane, though she snorted her dislike of the smoke and made at once for the far end of the paddock. The hackneys were more difficult. They were good tempered enough but they did not know her so well. She had to search for a halter and coax them all the way, but she got them out at last and left them to join Pegeen. Now there was only Lady Celia's old cob, another awkward customer because his gentle owner had never really attempted to cross his will. Luckily he was frightened enough to be biddable and only too thankful to follow his companions into the cleaner air. Since Murdoch had taken the big black, Napoleon, into Wigtown, that was the lot.

And now that the job was done, of course, here came help. She turned eagerly if a little crossly to the dark hurrying figures that came through the mirk, an enquiry as to their progress on her lips. But the first man to reach her was not one of the Dorne grooms. It was the tinkler man that she and

Lady Celia had seen hanging about in the lane. Doubtless the tinklers had seen the fire from their camp and had come to help. At the same moment a hoarse voice behind her enquired in Doric accents, 'Is this the lassie?'

The tinkler grinned, teeth gleaming white in his dark face. 'Aye, that's her. And a fine chase she's led us. Easy now. We don't want her hurt. But make sure of her.'

A hard powerful arm was flung round Chantal and a rough hand went over her mouth. There was no chance to cry out, though she had belatedly recognised the tinkler when he grinned. One of Cousin Giffard's watchdogs, who once had herded her back to the house when she had tried to pass the gates. She fought and kicked, resisting with all her might, but she was only a girl and slight of build while the man who held her was immensely strong. She heard him give a gruff chuckle as though her struggles amused him.'

The pseudo tinkler said impatiently, 'Hurry up, man. We've to get her away before she's missed. You're not here for your own pleasuring. Give her a tap on the head to quiet her. But not too hard, mind. He wants her in good shape.'

Chantal heard the gruff voice say, 'Easy now, ma wee beauty. Lie ye still, so's ye'll not get hurt,' and renewed her struggles. The voice said on a note of apology, 'Don't seem right to go a-hitting of a lassie, and ye sae bonny, but it's an order, ye ken.'

Something struck her a stunning blow on the side of her head and her world vanished in a maelstrom of spinning bright lights.

Nine

When she came to her senses she was in a carriage which, by the feel of it, was travelling fast. Someone had wrapped a heavy mantle over her evening gown. Her hands were lying in her lap but her wrists were tied and, for good measure, her arms had been lashed to her body so that she could not lift them to drag away the scarf that had been bound tightly over her face. She could scarcely breathe, let alone cry out, but she must have made some attempt at speech for a hoarse voice that she remembered all too well remarked on a note of satisfaction, 'That's the dandy, missy. Just you bide quiet a wee while and you'll soon feel more the thing. Got a headache, ain't you?'

She made no attempt at answer and her captor lapsed into silence. Gradually the pain in her head subsided, but she found if difficult to think clearly. The scarf-gag covered her eyes as well as her mouth so she could not tell whether she was being carried north or south, nor had she any idea how long she had been unconscious since she could not see the sky to estimate the time.

Her thoughts ran round and round like small trapped creatures vainly seeking some avenue of escape. All too easily she could guess the identity of the 'he' who wanted her 'in good shape'. How stupid she had been to have underestimated Cousin Giffard. Perhaps he had known her whereabouts from the beginning. It did not signify. At any rate he had allowed sufficient time to elapse to lull her into a false sense of security so that she had walked unsuspecting into his trap. Both Dominic and Murdoch had, she made no doubt, been lured away so that her abduction could be carried out with the least possible fuss. Her cousin had known her well enough to calculate that the threat to the horses would inevitably draw her out of the safe shelter of Dorne.

She wished that she knew what time it was and whether the alarm had been raised over her disappearance. Her dependence here was on Hilda, who would probably be the first to miss her. But no one would have a clue as to how she had vanished, still less where to start looking for her. And when it came to organising a search party they would be in sore difficulties. For the first time she regretted the lack of resident male servants at Dorne. Lady Celia found it simpler to manage with only female servants indoors, and until today Chantal had been inclined to agree with her. But now, with Dominic and Murdoch both absent that left only Bateson to come to her aid. She scarcely dared wonder what had happened to the grooms. It seemed unlikely that her cousin could have bribed them all to forsake their duty – some of them came of families that had served Dorne for generations – and surely he would not risk being involved in wholesale murder, but she feared that at best they must have been very roughly handled. So far as rescue was concerned she could see very little hope.

Chantal was a soldier's daughter, bred to keep a brave face when disaster struck, but even her courage quailed at the prospect before her. There would be no mercy at her cousin's hands. She had evaded him once. There would be no second chance. Then, with rescue ruled out of court, her only hope was to escape from her captors before they handed her over to him. Coldly, deliberately, she set herself to study the chances.

He would probably have fixed a rendezvous at some distance from Dorne – a distance that would make it appear impossible for him to have been implicated in her abduction. She certainly hoped so, since it would give her more time to effect her escape. Bribery was hopeless. She had no money with her and promises would have small value in the circumstances. Besides, no man who knew her cousin would dare play him false. His vindictive disposition was too well known. On the other hand she did not think her present guards bore her any particular ill will. The one who was sharing the coach with her had seemed quite sorry for his share in her misfortunes, though it had not stopped him from carrying out his orders. She was not too happy about the attitude of the other man – the one who had been sent to identify her and who was presumably driving the carriage. But if she was to have any hope of escape, the first requirement was to win free of her bonds. Would it be possible to persuade her present guard to take away the muffler? Even, perhaps, to free her hands.

She did not even know if he could see her, but she allowed her head to droop dejectedly against the squabs. And at least he must be able to hear her – unless he was asleep – so she essayed the effect of a few long-drawn shuddering sobs. She found it surprisingly easy to sob convincingly. It might be more difficult to stop.

Fortunately she was not obliged to persist for long in her efforts. The effect surpassed her hopes.

'Puir wee hen,' said the rough voice compassionately.

Inspiration prompted her to twist her bound wrists as though they pained her.

'Ye'd sit easier if ye were free o' they bonds,' ruminated the voice. 'And ye'll no risk jumping out o' the carriage and it going at this pace. Will you gi' me your promise that ye'll no raise riot and rumpus if I let ye loose?'

Chantal nodded vigorously and sought to compose her face into a suitably woebegone expression that belied rising spirits at this easy success. Clumsy hands wrestled with knots and pulled away the muffling scarf. She made a play of rubbing her wrists, which had not really been bound so cruelly tight, and thanked her benefactor in a husky, shaken little voice that required no acting ability at all and was quite unlike her usual clear confident tones.

He grunted. 'Aye. Ye've a bonny wheedling

way with you. But mind now, no mischief, or I'll have to tie ye up again,' and settled back into his corner averting his gaze from her as though he feared to be further beguiled.

She studied him surreptitiously as she rubbed and flexed her fingers and twisted about in her place as though to disperse the stiffness in her limbs. He was a giant of a man, as tall as Dominic and a good deal broader, with a rough-hewn craggy face and a thatch of reddish hair. The lines about the mouth seemed to indicate good humour, but the face, at the moment, wore a sullen expression as though he was ashamed of having been betrayed into showing kindness. If she did not tease him too far, he might serve her further, she thought.

She turned her attention to the passing scene, and was startled to discover that dawn was near. It must be four or five hours since she had been struck down. In that time they could have travelled a considerable distance, and her heart sank at the thought. From the lightening in the sky she judged that they were travelling roughly north-east, but the countryside was completely unfamiliar. She was sure that she had never seen it before, not even on her first journey north, but she dared not display too much interest in it, still less question the sullen giant. Her role must be that of crushed and helpless captive if she hoped to win further indulgence, and study of his expression suggested that she might now press her approach a little further.

'You were very kind to let me loose,' she told him shyly. 'I am much more comfortable now. Thank you. And I will be quiet, I promise.'

He grunted again, but he was obviously pleased. The sullen look vanished, to be replaced by an expression of guarded amiability, and presently he volunteered a remark of his own.

'We'll be stopping in a wee while to rest the horses and get a bite to eat. Ye'll be glad o' that, I daresay.'

Chantal's face blanched. 'My cousin?' she breathed, fixing huge frightened eyes on the man's face.

Again he was stirred to compassion. 'Nay, lass, nay,' he soothed, and actually leaned forward to pat her hand. 'No need to look like that. He'll not be there. Trust that careful customer to keep well out o' the way when there's risks to be run.'

She held his gaze steadily. 'When?' she said.

'Tonight,' he mumbled with equal simplicity. And the despair on the little white face so moved him that he added, on a burst of expletive incomprehensible to Chantal though its general sense was clear enough, 'Ah'd never ha' taken a hand in the business if Ah'd kenned ye were such a canny wee doo. But he's a hold on me, ye see, so we maun e'en thole it. Ah've a wife and a wee lassock to think of. Ah darena cross him.'

Chantal was aware of a faint flicker of pity for him, even in the midst of her own anxieties, but he seemed to be her only hope of escape and she could not afford to spare him for fear of what might be his fate at her cousin's hands. She asked about his little girl, and although she could not always understand his speech, gathered the impression that he was a devoted father. She wondered what crime he had committed that had given her odious cousin the power to blackmail him, for she was sure that money alone would never have persuaded him to the task. He seemed a kindly sort of man and plainly disliked the dirty business in which he found himself involved.

By the time that they stopped for breakfast the sun had risen and the oddly assorted pair in the carriage had established friendly relations, though Chantal was well aware that she must not trespass too far. The man's very virtues would prove her undoing. His devotion to his wife and child would prevent him from helping her escape. But at least he would grant her such measure of freedom as he considered safe, so long as he did not suspect her intention.

It was soon to be seen that her other jailer was of a very different kidney. He cursed vigorously at the discovery that Chantal was free of her bonds and rated Rab – the giant – for his folly in yielding to the girl's pleas.

'Nor she didn't ask me to,' growled Rab, the lowering expression of his brow promising trouble if he was baited further, 'not being in no case to talk, the way you'd gagged her. Said he wanted her well treated, didn't you? Why – she might well have choked to death.'

'And you an' me might well choke to death, me lad, if she gets away and raises the countryside,' retorted his fellow, illustrating his remarks with gruesome pantomime.

Rab winced, but put a bold face on it. 'She'll not do that, will ye, ma wee hen?' he said confidently.

Chantal smiled back at him. 'I have given my word that I will be quiet and biddable,' she said soberly, 'and I will keep it. It's Perkis, isn't it? Were you not long enough at the Court, Perkis, to learn that the Delaneys keep their promises? Though perhaps those who live there now are of a different breed.'

The man scowled angrily at her recognition. 'Hoity-toity ways'll do you no good here, milady. It's my turn to call the tune, and if I says you'll be tied up, tied up you'll be.'

'And if I says she won't, she won't,' announced Rab pugnaciously. 'She can come and break her fast with us. She'll be needing to stretch her legs, with a long day ahead of us, and you'll not tell me she can escape from two active men and both of them watching her every move.'

Perkis looked sour and resentful, but Rab was definitely a force to be reckoned with. If it came to fisticuffs he could pound the smaller man to a jelly, and Perkis knew it. He scowled, but he yielded.

Chantal was thankful enough to scramble out of the coach – unaided, because Rab was unused to such courtesies and Perkis would not so far demean himself. She looked about her curiously. The coach had been driven into the yard of a small deserted farmstead. It was plain that no one had lived here for years. In fact the roof was off, so Chantal could only be glad it was not raining. There was no furniture, and she wandered listlessly through the filthy mildewed rooms, peering through the grimy windows and finally seating herself on a low, deep window sill. The men went swiftly about their tasks. They had obviously been well drilled, for while Perkis saw to the horses and pumped water from the well, Rab lit a fire on the yawning hearth and brought in a hamper of provisions. For a man so large he was surprisingly neat and quick, and Chantal noticed with approval that after he had lit the fire he washed his hands before he handled the food. She wondered if it was his wife who had taught him to be so handy about the house. He hung a kettle on a hook over the fire and balanced a frying pan on the blazing logs. Cups and plates came out of the hamper and the hamper itself was used as a table. They had even remembered milk, thought Chantal in weary surprise, and recalled inconsequently the number of picnics when the milk, or some equally vital adjunct to the meal, had been forgotten.

She could not bring herself to eat the savoury smelling bacon that Rab presently brought her, though she managed a piece of bread and drank two cups of rather smoky tea with gratitude. Rab said apologetically that if she was sure she didn't want the food he would eat it himself since it was a pity to let good victuals waste. Perkis said nothing, but wolfed his portion in sour silence. When they had done eating Rab rinsed the plates and cups in a fresh bucket of water and re-packed the hamper, careful to remove every trace of their temporary occupation. Perkis obviously considered himself above this menial sort of work and sat smoking a pipe of rank-smelling tobacco while the fire smouldered down, from time to time taking out a large silver 'turnip' which he consulted ostentatiously. Rab, his task completed, beckoned Chantal outside and, in deep embarrassment, indicated a privy at the end of the derelict garden. Privy was something of a misnomer since the tumbledown shed lacked a door, and, 'I'm sorry, miss,' he mumbled, 'but I'll have to stay in the garden, case you was to take it into your head to run away. Not that there's anywhere to run to,' he ended thoughtfully, obviously thankful that his duties as a squire of dames had been satisfactorily accomplished.

Chantal could see that he was right. No

wonder the little farm had been deserted. The countryside was bleak, the soil thin and sour looking, with no sign of human habitation for miles, though somewhere she could hear the distant barking of a dog. No help to be found here. But the hot tea had banished the remnants of her headache and the argument between the two men, when Rab had taken her part, had done something to raise her spirits. Moreover the barking of that dog had given her the germ of an idea. She might not be able to contrive her own escape, but at least she could try to leave a trail that a possible search party might pick up. There was Jester. Neither her cousin nor his minions knew about Jester, or of the hound's amazing ability to follow a human scent. And surely Dominic would use the animal in his search? Because he *would* search for her. It never entered her head to doubt that.

In the optimistic mood induced by this tiny spark of hope, she began to count the obstacles that he would have to overcome. It must surely be evident that she had been carried off in some vehicle, and she thought it distinctly possible that the vehicle in question had been noticed, however careful her cousin's arrangements. It was not sufficient to dress Perkis in a sober coachman's livery and to select a carriage so nondescript as to pass unnoticed on a busy highway. They were not using a busy highway, and the party also included Rab, whose size alone would make him memorable.

Chantal, who was beginning to understand the country folk among whom she had passed the summer, thought it very likely that the strangers had been not only noticed but carefully studied and thoroughly discussed. No one would have questioned them directly – that would have been discourteous – but the purpose of their visit would have been the subject of much surmise, especially if they had been more than a day or two in the neighbourhood. A sparsely populated area might make abduction easy, but it was much more difficult to cover one's tracks in a district where everyone knew everyone else and most of them were related. Cousin Giffard would not have allowed for *that!*

So she was quite grateful when Perkis, making the most of his brief interlude of power, decreed that they would not start for another quarter of an hour. She put the time to good use, drifting about the desolate farmhouse with a depressed and nervous air which appeared to give Perkis considerable satisfaction and which allowed her to finger doors and window ledges as evidence of her abstraction. No bloodhound worthy of the name could possibly miss the scent of Chantal Delaney in that miserable hovel by the time she had done. Her final triumph was to succeed in handling the gate that gave access to the yard. While Perkis was harnessing up – and arguing with Rab about the desirability of tying her up again – she managed, on the pretext of a loosened shoe-string, to rest her foot on the bottom bar of the gate as she re-tied it. A well-simulated stumble as the foot came down allowed her to catch at a higher bar with both hands and to brush her skirts against the structure. Then she was ordered back into the coach, Rab looking morose again and warning her savagely that if there was so much as a peep out of her, he'd put her to sleep so's she'd not wake up till journey's end. But once again his humanity had prevailed over his partner's petty spite. She could only be thankful and sit meekly in her corner wondering what excuse she could make to be permitted to set foot on the ground again. It was a dispiriting task.

Once they stopped for a change of horses, but Rab took no chances. He pulled down the blinds and came to sit beside her, one powerful arm pinning her against his side, the other hand over her mouth.

'Might ha' been tempted ayont your strength,' he muttered, half surly, half apologetic, as he released her again.

About mid-afternoon they stopped again, this time to consult a road book. They had come to a cross-road, and the route that Perkis wished to follow looked very rough and narrow. After careful consultation he decided to chance it and was justified when, after about a mile and a half, it joined a much better road. The rough lane, it appeared, was a short cut to a newly made highway. Perkis studied this dubiously and backed the carriage into the mouth of the lane.

'Too much traffic for my liking,' he told Rab. 'Look at them wheel tracks! What do you say we back up a piece? I've a fancy for one o' those cold sausages and a sup of ale, but it'll not do to be hanging about on the high road.'

Rab's large frame demanded a good deal of sustenance. He was always ready to fall in with any suggestion that involved eating, so he was prompt to approve. The carriage was pulled up where the lane widened a little, and Perkis joined the other two in the interior. They ate in silence, for Perkis's presence inhibited any friendliness that Rab might have shown. The two men made a hearty meal. Chantal drank some of the milk left over from breakfast and ate some fragments of oatcake, choking down the dry morsels with a vague notion that she should make an effort to keep up her strength rather than because she had any appetite.

Perkis wiped greasy fingers on the seat of his breeches and jumped down into the lane, disappearing behind the hedge for a few moments. He came back presently and nodded to Rab, who also vanished briefly. Perkis leaned against the door of the carriage.

It was a loathsome necessity, but it was the chance she had been seeking and Chantal did not propose to miss it from any notions of pride or foolish modesty. With every appearance of embarrassment and looking anywhere but at Perkis's face, she muttered shamefacedly, 'May *I* go, too, please?'

Rab returned in time to hear Perkis guffaw. 'Aye, milady. All made the same way, ain't we? Got to answer nature's call or suffer for it, fine lady and 'umble groom alike,' he sniggered. But Rab's return and the scowl on the big man's face as he caught the tenor of the exchange prevented further taunts. A crimson-faced Chantal looked up pleadingly at Rab and indicated a gateway and a clump of bushes. He nodded. Perkis said sourly, 'And no trying to make a run for it. Five minutes. Then I'll be seeking you with this,' and he showed her the pistol that slipped so easily into the large pocket of his driving coat.

She wasted no time. Purposely she fumbled with the gate, then hurried behind the bushes. A strip torn from her handkerchief was tied to one low branch, and with the heel of her shoe she scratched a large arrow in the turf to indicate the direction they were taking. She was back beside the carriage within the allotted time and resumed her place in silence, ignoring Perkis's grin and his insolent enquiry as to whether she was more comfortable now.

To speak the truth she was very much more comfortable. If, by any combination of miracle and perseverance, a search party reached this point; she had left a plain and unmistakeable clue for them to find. The knowledge sustained her spirits until afternoon slowly gave place to evening. There had been no further opportunity to leave the carriage, and though they had passed several other vehicles and even one or two pedestrians on this more frequented road there had been no chance of eluding Rab's vigilance. Lights were beginning to prick out in the farmhouses and cottages that she could see tucked away in the folds of the hills. Evening was closing in, and with evening would come the encounter with her cousin. Despite her brave efforts, help might never reach her. With the coming of darkness it did not seem so certain that someone would have noticed the strange carriage, while the idea of Dominic using Jester in the search for her was probably ridiculous. The clues she had left – had abased herself to leave – were useless. Dominic was probably trotting peacefully home from Ayr, unless he had been delayed, and would not even know that she was missing. It was with sick foreboding that she realised that the carriage was passing through a gateway and proceeding up a neglected drive towards a squat, unpretentious house dimly seen in the dusk, where one lighted window proclaimed that they were expected.

Ten

But Dominic was not on his way home from Ayr. He had never even reached that historic town. He had left Dorne in a mood of dissatisfaction, not to say irritability. This he had ascribed largely to the fact that Chantal had disappeared somewhere in the grounds and that he had been unable to bid her farewell and remind her of the need to be cautious when she left the island. Telling himself that this was sheer folly did nothing to alleviate the heaviness of his spirits. He put Rusty into a hand gallop along the grassy verge. The exercise served to steady the headstrong animal but did nothing for his master. With every stride that separated him from Chantal his apprehension grew. He tried to convince himself that it was without foundation; merely the echo of his own foolish fears; the heritage bequeathed to him by that distant highland ancestress who, reputedly, had been blessed – or cursed – with the 'sight', but he was prey to the gloomiest forebodings. Some danger, some evil, threatened the girl he loved. It was no use telling himself that she was in safe keeping. With the best will in the world, Oliver was incapable of protecting her. Murdoch was a tower of strength, a good man with his hands and useful with a pistol if it came to shooting. But Murdoch was a busy man with many calls upon his services that might take him away from Dorne. Why had he not thought to tell Murdoch not to leave the island until his own return?

In an attempt to suppress his fears he deliberately turned his thoughts to the letter that was taking him north. The exercise gave him no comfort. As he had said to Oliver, the letter was suspiciously smooth. The writer introduced himself as a fellow philanthropist – which had immediately set up all Dominic's prickles. His charities were his own business. Only Oliver and the men who helped to implement his wishes were in his confidence. Not even his mother knew the whole. So how had this oily character come to be so well informed? Some of his pensioners had relatives who occasionally visited them, and no doubt they might have talked – one could scarcely pledge them to secrecy – but even if a vague rumour of his activities had reached the writer of the letter by such channels as these, he must have gone to a deal of trouble in ferreting out the whole. If he, Dominic, had not been so preoccupied with his wooing of Chantal, he might have thought of this before.

The more he thought of it now, the more it troubled him. The letter described the applicant's case with touching pathos. He was, it seemed, a splendid fellow, honest and industrious and incredibly brave, keeping a cheerful countenance in the face of his terrible afflictions. He was totally blind and had lost a leg. So what was he industrious *at*, demanded a disbelieving little imp at the back of Dominic's mind. He had amassed considerable experience in such cases and he knew that finding suitable employment was perhaps the greatest problem that the men had to face. Not a relative in the world, the writer went on, and no pension, despite his years of gallant service.

Then how had he lived, wondered Dominic. There was no mention of the campaigns in which the man had served so gallantly, nor of the engagement in which he had come by his injuries or of the regiment in which he had served. Too easy to check, reflected the cynical philanthropist grimly.

He drew the lightly sweating Rusty to a halt and considered the possibilities. No one was appointed to meet him in Ayr. He preferred to descend on unknown applicants unannounced. One was more likely to come at the truth that way. So no one would be discommoded if he deferred his visit for a few days. And despite all his efforts the conviction was steadily growing within him that he was urgently needed at home. If it proved to be just a foolish fancy, he had little to lose. He would have his journey to start again – and next time he would make adequate arrangements so that he could travel with an easy mind. If his fears were well founded, then Pegasus himself would not be swift enough to carry him home.

He pulled out his watch. Rusty was not quite done but he had been ridden hard. If he could hire a decent hack he could be home by midnight. Chantal would be surprised, Oliver would laugh. He would not mind the laughter so he found them both safe.

He was fortunate with his hireling. It had not Rusty's speed, nor, for that matter, his awkward temper, but it was a strengthy beast with a good heart and willingly gave of its best. He pressed on steadily, nursing the animal as best he could in face of his ever-increasing urge to make haste, and came home to Dorne a little before midnight. He slid out of the saddle at the end of the lane, encouraging the weary beast with heartening promises of clean straw and cool water and a feed of oats as a reward for its efforts, but even as he talked his nostrils were assailed by the acrid tang of a recent fire, and almost at the same moment he realised that all the horses were loose in the paddock. The stables! So that was the danger that he had sensed from afar. But the horses were all right. With a great sigh of relief that it was no worse, he turned the newcomer into the nearest loose-box and hurried round the corner of the building to discover the extent of the damage.

He walked into a scene that looked like a field hospital. The three grooms who lived in the quarters were stretched out on the ground, two of them unconscious and wrapped in blankets, the third groaning with the pain of a broken arm which Oliver was splinting for him. Oliver himself was a shocking sight. His clothes were soaked. His fine white evening shirt was caked with sand and blood, its sleeves in ribbons which revealed the cuts and bruises that covered his arms. But it was the set, white face, the glittering eyes, that most appalled his brother. Not since they had told him that he would never walk again had Oliver looked so. For one brief moment as he glanced up from his task and saw Dominic, a flicker of relief showed through the mask, but he said only, 'I thought it was Murdoch. He's gone to rouse the village.' He secured the bandage neatly, handed the patient a measure of brandy and bade him swallow it, assuring him that he would do very well in a little while and that the doctor would give him something to ease the pain when he arrived. Then he turned again to Dominic.

'My chair is over there,' he gestured. 'Murdoch fetched it over for me. But I've managed well enough without.' He glanced dispassionately at his arms. 'Bring it for me, will you? I've a tale to tell that is for your ear alone.'

At his request Dominic lifted him into the chair and wheeled him out of the circle of light cast by the stable lanterns down to the edge of the water. There, in the quiet darkness, his eyes fixed on the surge and ebb of the little waves, Oliver told his brother of Chantal's disappearance.

'I didn't know what was happening,' he

explained. 'One cannot hear very much down here. Certainly I didn't hear her cry out. She was busy about the horses for a while – I saw Pegeen at the bottom of the paddock. When she didn't come back to the boat and no one came with a message, I grew anxious. I managed to roll out of the boat – rolled *it* over, too, I'm afraid – and swam for the beach. Made what shift I could to drag myself up to the coach house and was just catching my breath after *that*, when Murdoch came clattering down the lane. *He* suspected mischief as soon as he discovered he'd been lured off to Wigtown on a wild goose chase. Horse thieves, he was thinking of, with those tinklers camping in the glen, but never dreamed of anything so shocking as this. We found the grooms easily enough. The first two had been knocked out as they slept, but that poor little devil must have roused. He'd put up a good fight against odds and taken a proper mauling. Arm, collar bone and a broken jaw, but he managed to mumble out something about a giant of a man, a stranger in these parts, and some of the tinklers from the camp. Murdoch fetched the others out here because the quarters are full of smoke and then went across to rouse the house and fetch my chair. Now he's away for the doctor and to get more help.'

There was a heavy silence. Then he added slowly, 'I'm sorry, Nick. I should have guarded her better.'

In the darkness Dominic's hand dropped on his shoulder with a comforting pressure. 'Not your fault, old fellow. I had grown careless. Too busy planning how I could win her to wife to remember the danger in which she stood. But tomorrow will be time enough for apportioning blame and repentance. Tonight we've to plan how to get her back.'

There were lights bobbing towards them down the lane. They must go back and see to the comfort of the injured grooms before they could give their full attention to the far more difficult task of tracing Chantal. It was late indeed before they had made the best arrangements that could be contrived for the casualties and were able to foregather in Murdoch's office for a council of war. Murdoch begged leave to introduce to this one, George Crawford, the son of a neighbouring farmer. 'For Geordie and me ha' noticed twa-three queer-like things that'll maybe help,' he explained, for once forgetting the meticulous English that he normally used in his dealings with his employers.

Considered as a rescue party, they were a sorry crew. Oliver had been harried into changing his sodden clothes, but since Bateson had insisted on anointing his hurts with some much-vaunted ointment he wore a dressing gown over his shirt and breeches. Both Dominic and Murdoch had spent long hours in the saddle as well as enduring anxieties that could scarcely be assessed, while Geordie Crawford had done a long day's work in the harvest field. All of them showed it. And all of them showed in a far greater degree a marked determination to make someone pay for the damage that had been done. When it presently emerged that the young groom who had suffered the most in the attack was Crawford's cousin, they seemed to be linked more closely than ever in their common aim.

'Let's have your report first then, Murdoch,' began Dominic crisply, 'since you seem to have noticed more than the rest of us.'

'Nay. 'Twas what Geordie said that set me to thinking,' demurred the steward. 'His uncle keeps an inn, a quiet sort of place, mostly used by the herds and drovers and a few farm folk. Not a house that's patronised by the gentry. But a gentleman *did* stop there – 'bout three weeks back, Geordie reckons it would be. His uncle can tell us for sure. He didn't stay above an hour or so – just asked if the goodwife could dish him up some kind of a meal and a bite for his man. Which she did, though not accustomed to such. Only while his chops were broiling, the pair of them strolled out down the lane and were gone half an hour so that the meat was scorched. Geordie's aunt was in a rare taking, because she rates herself a good plain cook. Why couldn't the gentleman have sat in the coffee room and drunk a tankard of home-brewed like a Christian, she wanted to know, instead of stravaiging about the lanes while good food spoiled. Then, just a week ago, back comes the same carriage and the same coachman, though no gentleman this time. The man – Perkins, Geordie says he's called, or something like that – says can the landlord house the carriage and stable the horses for a few days. He has business in the neighbourhood, but it's with the outlying farms where there's no carriage roads so shanks's pony will have to serve. Geordie's uncle agreed to it and even offered him the loan of his old garron, but the fellow said he was no horseman and would manage as best he might. They'd have thought no more of it, but Geordie chanced to see him coming away from the tinklers' camp and wondered what sort of business he could have there. 'Twasn't till I happened to say to Geordie that they were a queer sort of tinklers that were camping in the glen that *he* said, "Aye. And they keep gey queer company," didn't you, Geordie lad?'

Drawn thus into the centre of the stage, Geordie crimsoned but nodded vigorously.

Dominic waited patiently. Best let the pair come at the story in their own fashion. If he tried to hurry them they might get flustered and omit some vital detail. And that queer sixth sense of his was telling him that they were on the right track. 'And then?' he said steadily.

Murdoch rubbed his lean jaw ruminatively. 'Two days agone that was,' he decided. 'And tonight, as I was turning on to the coast road, a strange carriage passed me, coming from Glenluce. And by what I can make out it sounds the dead spit of the one that Geordie spoke of. A neat plain job, painted dark blue, and nothing to distinguish it from a dozen others, but drawn by a well-matched pair of Cleveland bays, just such as the lad described. I couldn't make out the driver in the darkening, but it took the Wigtown road.'

Dominic sprang to his feet, scarcely able to believe that the first throw of the dice had fallen their way, and equally unable to contain his urge to be off at once in pursuit.

'The tinklers' camp first,' he planned aloud. 'If they were the ones who attacked the stables, they'll be gone. Then to your uncle's inn, Geordie. Could you undertake to recognise that carriage again, even if they've changed horses?'

Geordie shook his head dubiously, but was understood to say that he'd do his best. 'It had green silk curtains with a yellow and white fringe,' he suddenly remembered, and brightened considerably.

'If we can get near enough to see those, I'll not cavil at the colour scheme,' said Dominic grimly. 'Can your father spare you to go with us? I'd not ask it, so busy as he'll be while the good weather lasts, but you are the only one of us who has actually seen the carriage by daylight.'

Geordie was quite sure that his father would raise no objections to his joining in the hunt. He clearly felt that he had fallen in with high adventure and was not disposed to miss any of it.

Oliver said slowly, 'You're not fit to set out tonight, Nick. None of us is.' And at the impatient jerk of his brother's head he smiled a little sadly. 'And well I know you can't endure to wait. Well – here's a notion for you. Take the carriage. Oh yes – Pegeen as well, of course. And a couple of hacks if you can lay hands on them. Geordie's father's got a useful sort of hunter that's the right style. Remember they've a long start, even if we've guessed right. This is going to be a gruelling chase, and it won't just be a case of pounding hell for leather after them. Heaven knows where they're heading for, so we can't be sure where they'll turn off, but we can lay to it that they'll use by-roads where they can. We'll need all our wits about us if we're to pick up their trail. In the carriage we can take it in turns, one to drive and one to rest, while the others scout ahead and to the sides. We can't keep a close formation – the carriage is bound to fall behind if the riders are on a hot scent, but it can catch up when the horsemen check.'

It was a sensible plan. It might slow them down a little but it would give them a wider field of search. And Oliver's careless use of hunting terminology put Dominic in mind of another possible ally.

'And Jester,' he said. 'She can't track a carriage. But they're bound to stop somewhere, and if Chantal is allowed to set foot to ground, Jester will tell us. And she can rest in the carriage in between whiles.'

Murdoch also lent support to the plan, pointing out that in the carriage they could carry a supply of food so that they need stop only for the necessary changes of horses, and Dominic, recalling the theory of a famous soldier that an army marches on its stomach, rather reluctantly consented to the further slight delay.

He made one attempt to persuade his brother to stay behind. Oliver gave him a wry grin. 'If you could persuade me that I would be a hindrance, you should have your way,' he said quietly. 'As it is, remember that I can drive as well as any of you, even if I *do* have to be lifted on to the box. And it was I who gave her into the hands of her enemies. Do you still want to hold me back?'

And Dominic yielded without further argument and went to look out his pistols. Half an hour later they were on their way.

Eleven

Perkis finished counting the money and stowed it away in an inner pocket.

The Honourable Giffard Delaney fumed in impotent fury. 'Satisfied?' he demanded in biting tones. The insolence of it! The fellow actually checking to see that he had not been bilked. As well that this pair were bound for the Americas where such revolutionary notions might be tolerated.

Perkis nodded sullenly. He wished he dared voice his opinion of his employer. A fine one *he* was to be putting on superior airs, and him kidnapping his own cousin. Reckoning to rape her, too, and force her into wedlock that way, unless Perkis missed his guess. Why else should he have appointed a rendezvous at this lonely spot, and never another soul in the house? Not that he'd any sympathy for the girl. She was another of the high-nosed kind. But still!

'Then you can take yourselves off. You'll need all your time. The Irish packet sails on the evening tide. You'll be met in Stranraer as we arranged so that you can hand over the gig. Your family will also join you in Stranraer, Kennedy,' he added, turning briefly to Rab. 'And I would advise you both to forget that you ever saw Glenluce or the island of Dorne. Your future lies overseas. It would be, shall we say, unhealthy, for you to contemplate a return to your native shores.'

The voice was practically expressionless, but neither man doubted that he meant what he said. They did not linger over their departure. Only Rab Kennedy spared a pitiful thought for that poor lass whom he had helped to deliver to the mercies of such a man. But what choice had he had? He decided that at the first opportunity he would burn a candle to Saint Jude on her behalf.

The Honourable Giffard, meanwhile, busied himself with certain domestic duties to which he was completely unaccustomed. The girl would keep. Indeed she would be all the better for keeping. A salacious smile curved the loose mouth as he imagined the mental torment that she must even now be suffering. She was safe enough, locked in that small closet that had a window so narrow that not even a child could have forced an entry. And the key was in his pocket. He patted it lovingly.

He proceeded to make up the fire and to push a shabby couch in front of it. The house which he had hired was cold from long disuse, the bedrooms so damp as to be unfit for habitation. No matter. This one room would serve. For both of them, he reflected, gloating.

He set bread and cold meats and wine on a table whose polished surface was marred by the bloom of damp, and drew up two chairs. Having surveyed the result of his labours, he added a basket of fruit before pulling out his watch, since the clock on the mantel shelf did not go, and deciding that his hour had come. His captive would be exhausted and frightened and weak with hunger since he had been told that she had eaten practically nothing all day. Well – she could eat now, if she'd a mind for it. And he would explain to her exactly how matters stood.

Chantal followed him into the firelit room quietly enough. She had explored the closet as best she could in the dark and had realised that it offered no possibility of escape. Nor could she endure the thought of being dragged out bodily like some cowering animal if she disobeyed. But she refused to sit down and declined her cousin's offer of refreshment.

He shrugged. 'As you wish, my dear. You'll be glad enough of rest and food presently.'

She managed to repress a shiver. 'Shall I? What do you propose to do with me, cousin?'

He smiled and poured himself a glass of wine. 'Oh, come now! You're not so innocent as that,' he mocked, sipping appreciatively. 'I think you know very well the delights that are in store for us. Here we are, just the two of us, in our love nest with none to hinder us or intrude upon our bliss. The furnishing is a little Spartan, I grant you, but I promise that my ardour shall make amends. By tomorrow, my love, I think you will gladly consent to our marriage. For your own sake one must hope so. Obduracy would be unwise. This is a lonely spot. There would be no one to hear your – er – protests, should it prove necessary to school you to submission as I do my horses.' He nodded significantly at the whip that lay on the mantel shelf. 'For the ceremony itself there is no particular hurry. Illicit delights are sweetest, and you have much to learn before I carry you to

Gretna, where we shall be wed in the most romantic fashion. Is not that a delightful prospect?'

It was a prospect that made Chantal feel physically sick, and it was all the more bitter for that careless mention of Gretna and the remembered happiness that it evoked. And so far as she could see there was no hope of rescue or escape. Her cousin might not have the physique of a Rab Kennedy, but he was quite strong enough to force a girl to his will. The best she could do for herself was to delay the inevitable as long as possible. With shaking hands and a pathetically white face she seated herself at the table. But though her coward body might betray her, her spirit was still unbroken.

'It seems I shall have need of all my strength, cousin,' she told him steadily. 'The prospect of such favour is almost too much for me. So perhaps, after all, I will take wine with you.'

He tittered, a greedy note in the unpleasant sound. 'Brava!' he approved condescendingly. 'That's more like it. I prefer a filly with spirit. I daresay we shall deal extremely together. I shall teach you how to please me – an exacting task, for I am not easily satisfied, but there is no need for haste. I was a little annoyed with you, you know, for putting me to so much trouble and expense. It was very foolish of you to run away. I am not so easily thwarted. Now you must pay forfeit for your wilfulness. It will be most enjoyable,' he told her dreamily, gazing into the ruby heart of his wine glass. 'In fact when I recall all the discomforts I have endured this month past, I feel it may well take some time to purge you of your naughtiness. It is a sad pity that, in the end, I shall be forced to marry you. You understand, of course, that only the need to secure your fortune drives me to so extreme a measure. But you shall beg me to do so. Yes. That is it. By the time I am done with you, you shall beg me, on your knees, to legalise our union, just as you shall learn to bring me the whip and acknowledge that you stand in need of correction.'

She sickened anew. Somehow she forced herself to raise the wine glass to her lips and sip a little of its contents. It would not do, though, to be drinking too much of this potent stuff without eating, even if she had to choke down every mouthful. She drew the dish of meat towards her and made a careful selection.

Eating was even more difficult than she

had feared. She managed to swallow a mouthful or two, pushed the rest about on her plate and crumbled a piece of bread. Presently, with a deep, unconscious sigh, she pushed the plate away and took a peach from the basket of fruit. Perhaps that would prove easier to swallow. She made a long business of peeling and quartering it. Cousin Giffard, his own meal long finished, sat and watched her and secretly exulted. Let her employ her delaying tactics. They would not serve. And every moment of delay would only increase the fear and the tension that she was striving so hard to conceal. Small clumsinesses betrayed her. He smiled when a piece of fruit slipped from her shaking fingers and when she spilled a few drops of wine.

But this satisfaction soon palled. He wanted to see terror start in her eyes as she realised that her fate was inevitable; to feel the slim warm body struggling hopelessly against his greater strength; to hear her whimpers for a mercy that he would not grant. He got up abruptly, regardless of the forms of courtesy, and strolled over to the hearth, his fingers playing suggestively with the thong of the whip.

Chantal's heart leapt in sheer panic. She

had seen already that there was nothing in the room that she could use as a weapon. There were the table appointments, but with his eyes upon her there was no hope of secreting a knife, and little use, either, since they were of silver and far from sharp. Nor were there any fire irons. It was a log fire and needed no poker. There was the whip on which his fingers were resting. If she could get hold of that – trick him into thinking her so sunk in terror that she had no thought of attack – she might be able to bring down the butt on his head with sufficient force to stun him. The door was not locked. Perhaps she could escape from the house and hide in the darkness. Any scheme, however wild, was better than waiting here in helpless dread.

She put down her wine glass and rose, and Giffard came forward with mock courtesy to draw back her chair. Chantal crossed to the hearth and stood with one hand resting on the mantel shelf and the other stretched out to the flickering flames. He came to stand beside her but he did not touch her. Instead he permitted his glance to rove over her slender body, savouring the delights in store. Even in her fear and her dishevelment – for she had been granted no opportunity to tidy her person since she had been snatched from Dorne – she was very lovely. Perkis had taken away the travelling mantle before he handed her over to his master, and the diaphanous evening gown that she wore had been designed to draw attention to its wearer's femininity. It left the white throat and beautifully moulded shoulders exposed to that greedy stare, and gently emphasized the delicious curves of breast and thigh. Giffard heaved a long shuddering sigh of rapt anticipation and stepped forward to take her in his arms.

She took a pace backward, and her fingers touched the thong of the whip, but before she could grasp it he had seized her in a crushing embrace, one arm holding her pressed against his body while his free hand caressed her throat and shoulder and slid down her spine to stroke and squeeze her thigh and his mouth fastened rapaciously on hers so that she could scarcely breathe.

She twisted and writhed in his hold but it was useless. It was not until he himself slackened his grasp a little that she was able to turn her head away for a moment. She caught at the edge of the mantel shelf so that her fingers brushed the whip stock, but allowed her head to droop dejectedly and drew long, gasping breaths, feigning a weakness and giddiness that drew a triumphant laugh from her cousin.

'Too hot for you, my love?' he jibed. 'That is because you are over-dressed for the business and may soon be mended.' He caught hold of her dress at the shoulder and ripped the fragile fabric from neck to waist.

'That's more like it,' he said a little thickly, and the predatory hand fondled her bosom.

Chantal snatched up the whip and brought it down with all her strength. She aimed to strike him on the head, but alas! As the blow descended he stooped to kiss her again. The whip stock slid harmlessly past his head and struck him a painful blow on the shoulder, while the lash flicked back across his face and cut his cheek. He sprang back, releasing her for a moment as his hand flew up to his face, then closed with her again, wresting the whip from her grasp and tossing it on to the couch.

'That was not wise,' he said softly, venomously. 'Such forward behaviour merits sharp punishment. But it poses a pretty problem. Shall I administer that punishment at once, or shall I possess you first? I think perhaps, on the whole, the punishment will keep.'

'Now that is just where you are mistaken,' said Dominic quietly from the doorway. 'The punishment is just about to begin.'

He was across the room in two fierce strides to seize Chantal's assailant by his beautifully tailored coat collar and swing him away from her, while the girl herself was overwhelmed by the recognition of a delighted Jester who had sought her long and patiently.

There was not much science about the opening phase of the combat that followed. Neither contestant was a notable exponent of the noble art, though both had learned something of its principles as part of the education proper to a gentleman. For one or two anxious moments, as she watched the fierce flurry of blows, Chantal actually wondered if her champion, even though he had arrived in time, might not yet be defeated, for it seemed to her that Cousin Giffard was the more active of the two, with Dominic concerned rather to block his attack than to take the initiative. But as the grim struggle went on, Giffard's breath began to come in gasps and there was sweat standing in great beads on his forehead. His attempts to land a telling blow grew wilder, feebler. Again and again he left chin and mark unguarded. Had Dominic not been imbued by a vengeful fury, determined to exact a heavy penalty for all that his little love had undergone, he could have ended it a good deal sooner. As it was, both Murdoch and Geordie had arrived and were standing in the doorway before he made an end, and so were privileged to witness what the enthusiastic if untaught Geordie later described to his father as 'the prettiest left hook to the mark that a man could wish to see.'

Having vented his fury, Dominic looked down at the huddled heap with acute distaste and brushed his hands together as though to rid them of some foul contamination. Then he raised his head and looked at Chantal.

Neither spoke. He simply held out his arms and Chantal walked straight into them. Regardless alike of her own appearance and of the interested audience in the doorway, she held up her face for his kiss in the most natural way and, as he gathered her close, gave a great sigh of contentment and put up her hands to frame his face and returned his kisses with every sign of pleasure.

A delighted Geordie nudged Murdoch, who, recalled to a sense of propriety, took him firmly by the arm and led him back into the entrance hall. But Murdoch, too, was a-grin with delight. Now they would do, he thought contentedly. There would be a wedding, with all the age-old ritual of celebration that attended the marriage of a Merriden. A ritual in which Murdoch's heart delighted. And in good time there would be heirs, to care for Dorne in the years to come. She was a gallant little lass, the way she had taken thought to leave a trail for them, and herself terrified out of her wits as she must have been. She should bear sturdy sons.

The lady herself had no thought for the future. The present was happiness enough. Gone were all her doubts, all her resentment of the submission required from a wife. In one simple gesture she had given herself and her future into Dominic's hands and it was for him to do with her as he wished. Nor did Dominic recall the formal phrases in which he had planned to propose marriage. His thought was all for the comforting of the shaken, weary girl in his arms. She had suffered the most shocking indignities, and largely through his carelessness, he thought remorsefully. Though he would guard and cherish her for the rest of his days, he would never wholly forgive himself.

He smoothed his lips gently over her soft cheek, pressed one more kiss on her mouth, and put her a little away from him, yet keeping his hands on her shoulders as though he could not endure to have her out of his hold.

'Try to forget,' he said gently. 'There is nothing more to fear, and we'll have you out of here as soon as you've changed your dress.'

She looked up, startled. 'My dress?' she said wonderingly. And for the first time looked down at herself and realised the appearance that she presented. 'Oh!' she said, on a gasp of horrified discovery. 'What *must* you think of me?'

That, at least, brought a smile to Dominic's lips. 'If I were to tell you, my darling, we should be here for some time. And since it is an object with us to get you away from this place before your presence here can be discovered, perhaps I had best leave that question until we are at leisure.'

She blushed furiously and tried to pull the torn edges of her gown into a semblance of decency, but he told her not to fret over that since Hilda had packed a portmanteau with everything that she might need. 'And was sorely put about because we refused to bring her along with us,' he added. 'But there simply wasn't room for her. Do you wait here, sweetheart, and I will bring it for you, and get Geordie to remove that – that corruption,' he finished carefully, selecting this term, of all those that sprang to mind, as being best suited to a lady's ears.

At Chantal's suggestion the Honourable Giffard was bundled away in the small closet where she herself had been imprisoned.

''Twill do him no harm to come to his senses in yon hole and think himself locked in to perish o' hunger and thirst,' said the vengeful Murdoch in satisfied tones.

Dominic nodded entire agreement with these sentiments. 'We'll throw the key through the window before we go,' he elaborated. 'Let him scrabble around in the darkness before he finds it.'

He brought Chantal a bowl of water and soap and a towel. She made a hasty but adequate toilet in front of the fire, scrambling thankfully into a neat travelling dress of bronze-green corded silk and pulling a hooded cloak over it. She pushed her torn dress and soiled linen into the portmanteau, taking care that not so much as a hairpin was left behind to betray her brief occupation.

There was not much she could do about her hair, but she coiled it up as smoothly as possible and drew the hood over it.

Dominic, at any rate, seemed well pleased with her appearance when he came tapping at the door to know if she was ready. He snatched a quick kiss and told her that she was 'a grand lass to ride the waters with' which, on the Borders, is a compliment of no mean order. Then he hurried her out to the waiting carriage.

With Murdoch driving and Geordie riding escort, the occupants of the vehicle were able to exchange notes on their adventures, though Dominic insisted that the full story must keep till the morrow. Chantal must rest. He regretted the discomfort that she must suffer from trying to sleep in a fast moving carriage but if possible he wanted her safe back in Dorne before morning broke. All of them were weary. They would take it in turns to rest and would do their best to disturb her as little as possible when they changed places. Did she not think that she could make herself reasonably comfortable propped in a corner with her feet on the opposite seat?

Chantal was sure she wouldn't be able to sleep a wink, but at least she could put up a good pretence of slumber so that they would not worry over her. 'But there's just one thing,' she said hesitantly. She really didn't like to mention it, with Dominic so concerned over making haste, but, 'I suppose you haven't anything to eat,' she ventured. 'I'm starving of hunger.'

Dominic hugged her and laughed. 'My precious, beloved brat!' he exclaimed. 'Do you know, that was almost the first thing you ever said to me? All these months since Jester and I fished you out of the water, and you're still falling into scrapes and then demanding to be fed! Well – thanks to Murdoch – this time the commissariat is better supplied. Last time I had to sacrifice my own lunch and sorely I begrudged it since I'd been up since dawn and was devilish sharp-set. What's more we have an excellent cordial known to the natives as "malt". I think – don't you, Noll – that a small measure, suitably diluted with water, might help to induce sound sleep.'

Oliver was rummaging in a hamper from which he presently produced some portions of cold chicken, an apple pie, rather battered from its travels, and a large hunk of cheese. It was difficult to eat tidily when one was being jolted and bounced over a rough road, but Chantal did not know when food had tasted better. The 'cordial' which Dominic obliged her to swallow when at last her hunger was appeased made her throat sting and her eyes water but was wonderfully warming and comforting when it got down inside. It made her drowsy, too, so that she allowed him to tuck her up in the carriage rugs without further protest.

Whether it was the effect of the cordial or just natural exhaustion, she slept the night through, rousing occasionally when they stopped to change places, vaguely aware of the men's lowered voices but drifting off to sleep again without so much as opening her eyes. When at last she did open them it was to find Dominic smiling down at her and bidding her rouse, for they were back at Dorne and she must try to walk down to the boat.

'Not that I wouldn't gladly carry you,' he added, 'but we are rather later than I had hoped and we want to appear as commonplace as possible, just in case there is anyone astir, so it would be better if you could walk.'

It was a full day, with the sunlight glittering on the blue waters of the bay. Walk? Chantal felt more inclined to dance!

And there, across the smiling water, was Dorne, beckoning to a future in which she would become more and more a part of it.

Twelve

Lady Celia, displaying a determination in marked contrast to her usual vague gentleness, decreed that they should all retire to bed. Yes, of course she was longing to hear the story, but for the moment it was sufficient that they were safe home again. The details would keep, and she had no desire to have three invalids on her hands. The men were not unwilling, though they protested about unnecessary feminine fuss. Chantal, who felt perfectly rested and refreshed, begged off, saying that what she needed far more than sleep was a hot bath. In the primitive conditions obtaining at Dorne, hot baths were something of a luxury, but Hilda soon had the maids scurrying about the task of preparing one. Since it was so early she even agreed to Chantal's request that her hair should be washed as well, since there would be plenty of time to dry it before bed time.

When her leisurely luxurious toilet was completed, save for her hair, which still lay in damp strands on her shoulders, Hilda surveyed her critically.

'If I may make so bold, miss, being abducted seems to suit you,' she said drily.

Chantal twinkled mischievously. 'Not being abducted,' she said. 'That was horrid. It was being rescued.' And betook herself to the terrace where she could let her hair dry in the sun and dream blissful dreams of a future as Dominic's wife.

Lunch was a happy meal. Lady Celia plied them with eager questions and Dominic committed the heinous crime of feeding Jester at table. Even the hound looked surprised, though it did not prevent her from accepting the succulent offering and making off with it before he could repent his unwonted indulgence. To the startled faces of his companions he explained, in guilty apology, 'I thought she had earned it. It was she who led us to the strip of linen that you had tied to the bush, and so showed us the pointer that indicated the way you had taken. If it had not been for that we might have cast north instead of south and so lost precious time.' He fell silent a moment, facing the implication of what he had just said, contemplating the horror that Chantal might have been called upon to endure, had they not saved those few vital moments, and, strong and happy and safe as he was, he too sickened and shuddered at the thought. But such torturing imaginings must be dismissed. Fate – or the luck – call it what you would – had been with them. He came back thankfully to the comfortable present.

It was not just Jester of course. Everyone had had a hand in their success, from Oliver, who had done most of the driving so that the rest of them could search, to Geordie, who had recognised a pair of weary Cleveland bays in the stable of a lonely inn and had engaged the ostler in conversation about them.

'That gave us a lead for the next stretch.'

Chantal's efforts to leave traces of her presence in the lonely farmstead had provided another gleam of relief. Dominic vowed he had lost count of the deserted, tumbledown buildings that they had searched in vain.

'We guessed they would probably stop to eat somewhere where the horses and the carriage could be hidden, and that it was unlikely they would use an inn except when a change of horses was necessary, but it was a soul-destroying business when every moment counted.'

Then Chantal must tell of her captors and of Rab Kennedy's kindness and how he had told her that his wife and child were going with him to America where they hoped to make a new start.

Dominic scowled. 'Queer sort of kindness,' he grunted. 'If it were not for the scandal I'd have the pair of them apprehended and brought back to stand trial.'

But Chantal cried out at that, saying that he might do what he liked about Perkis but she held no grudge against Rab.

'And you can't touch one without involving the other,' Oliver pointed out, 'besides the scandal. I devoutly trust that no one saw us come home this morning.'

'Why not?' asked Chantal, surprised.

'Because, my dear girl, we mean to put it about that we made a long excursion to visit Glen Trool, and while we might say that an accident to the carriage had delayed our return, it would be difficult to account for *quite* so long an absence,' explained Oliver patiently.

'We could say I was visiting friends in the neighbourhood,' suggested Chantal carelessly, 'though I really can't see that it signifies *where* I was.'

'We could say no such thing. And of

course it signifies,' said Dominic roundly. 'Haven't you learned yet that in this part of the world everybody knows everyone else? There would be immediate enquiry as to the identity of your friends. Not from idle curiosity, but because of the need to trace their pedigrees and decide in just what degree they were related to the local gentry. And as for not signifying, just get it into that innocent head of yours that it is your good name that is at stake. Because your cousin was responsible for your abduction we cannot tell the truth, yet we must account for your absence from Dorne – if word of it should get out – or you wouldn't have a shred of reputation left. Since you, and we, are well aware that you are an innocent victim, this may not seem to you of great account. But this is not London. Our neighbours are decent upright folk, the kindest you could wish to meet and the most generous. But where morals are concerned they are absolutely rigid. When we are married we shall want to spend a good deal of our time here. It would be extremely uncomfortable if every respectable female in the district refused to receive you.'

What Chantal might have replied was,

perhaps fortunately, lost, since Lady Celia put her oar in first. 'Oh! Are you going to be married?' she enquired, with just such an air of pleased interest as she might have displayed if they had announced their intention of going into Newton Stewart to look at the shops. 'How delightful! You won't forget to write and tell your mama, will you, Dominic? She will be *so* interested. And these small attentions, you know, are most gratifying as one grows older. *Do* try to remember.'

Dominic solemnly gave her the required assurance. But when she asked in a bewildered kind of way why Oliver and Chantal found her admonitions so amusing, the temptation was too much for him.

'I'm afraid they're laughing at me,' he told her gloomily. 'As you know, I've always taken good care to steer clear of matrimony. But this time I am fairly cornered. Obviously, after her recent escapade, *someone* must marry the girl. Chivalry insists upon that. And since I was responsible for bringing her here, all the laws of hospitality demand that I be the sacrifice. You will appreciate that, once I have informed my parents of my honourable intentions, my doom is sealed. In the bosom of my family I need not strive to conceal the deep dismay with which I view my approaching fate, but noblesse oblige, my dear aunt, and I hope to maintain a *resigned*, if not actually a *cheerful* countenance in the face of the world.'

At this point his promised bride picked up the apple which she had just selected and flung it at him. He fielded it neatly and bit into it with relish. 'Just what I wanted,' he declared, 'sweet and crisp with a touch of tartness.' And if the expression in the blue eyes gave the simple words a different significance, at least Chantal subsided, smiling across the table at him with her heart in her eyes for all the world to see.

Lady Celia shook her head and said that she did not think she would ever understand the modern generation.

'Isn't it going to be a trifle complicated?' asked Oliver thoughtfully, when his aunt had gone off to her own sanctum, declaring that she must look up the antecedents of the Delaney family so that she could incorporate Chantal's family tree into the Merriden history. 'I think you should be married as soon as possible' – a remark which met with unqualified approval from both his listeners – 'because only so will Chantal feel really safe. But she is not of age. And to be asking

Lord Hilsborough's permission to pay your addresses is rather an awkward business under the circumstances.'

Dominic looked grim. 'I shan't *ask*,' he said coldly. 'I shall inform his lordship that, with or without his permission, I propose to marry his ward, since he is apparently incapable of protecting her from the improper advances of his own son.'

Oliver held his peace. He could not wholly approve such abrupt dealing, however much his sympathies lay with his brother, since it held a faint flavour of blackmail. He said pacifically, 'It's odd, isn't it, how these black sheep appear from time to time in our best families? A throw-back, I suppose, to some scoundrelly ancestor. Hilsborough's older boy isn't at all a bad sort. Blockish, but good-hearted enough.' His eyes lit to pure mischief. 'It will be interesting, don't you think, to see what Aunt Celia makes of Chantal's progenitors?'

'I can guess what she'll find on the distaff side,' retorted Dominic promptly, his brow clearing. 'A long line of redoubtable females who kept castles for Crusading husbands or directed the defence of their homes against assault by Roundhead troops. Tough and dauntless.'

'So they had need to be if they chanced to have Merridens to deal with. For of all the stubborn, arrogant' – words failed her.

Dominic grinned delightedly. 'My sweet, submissive little love. Always ready to show hackle,' and pulled her into his arms and kissed her soundly, to the amusement of the watching Oliver. And Chantal wondered once more why it was that however he might tease and provoke, his touch, his kiss, could instantly disarm her, so that all she desired was to cling more closely in his hold and surrender herself to his love making.

They debated the question of their marriage both soberly and in frivolous mood during the week that followed. Apart from their morning rides neither Dominic nor Chantal left the island. For some reason they seemed to have no desire to seek distraction on the mainland. Aunt Celia was surely the most easy-going of chaperones and raised no objection when they disappeared for long hours at a stretch into a garden that offered a number of secluded corners where any argument could safely be brought to an amicable conclusion. And at the end of the week they were no nearer to reaching a decision about marriage plans than they had been at the beginning. Oliver, in a mood of levity, had even suggested a Gretna ceremony. Chantal shuddered, in a sickening surge of memory, and Dominic asked severely what good that would be. If the bride was under age her guardian could have such a marriage annulled if he so chose.

'And then, you know, she might not be able to bring me up to scratch again,' he pointed out blandly, seeing the stricken expression in Chantal's eyes and anxious, by any means to dispel it.

In a sparsely furnished parlour in an isolated house many miles from Dorne, another man was considering and rejecting possible marriage plans. But in the case of the Honourable Giffard, his selected bride was more than unwilling, which added to his difficulties. He was stretched at ease on the shabby couch with a bottle of brandy on the table beside him to aid the processes of thought, but he was still far from comfortable. He had spent a long period of abject terror locked in the closet, in the belief that he had been left there to starve to death and remembering that, as he had taken care to tell his victim, there would be no one to hear his cries for help. Since Dominic had found considerable satisfaction in closing the eyes that had dared to gaze upon Chantal's loveliness, it had been some time before he discovered the key. And since the mouth that had forced lascivious kisses on a defenceless girl had been smashed into something more nearly resembling a piece of raw steak than a human mouth, it was still longer before he was able to satisfy the gnawing ache of hunger with anything but liquids.

Stronger by far than the desire to possess himself of his cousin's lands and fortune was now the craving for revenge. But rack his brains as he would he could not devise a scheme that would deliver Chantal into his hands without any risk of detection. The element of surprise would be lacking, and his two helpful minions were by now on the high seas. He hoped they were suffering all the miseries of sea sickness, poured himself more brandy, and winced as the raw spirit stung his sore mouth.

Perhaps it was the brandy. Certainly the glimmering of an idea came to him. He turned it about thoughtfully. It was not perfect, not all that he would wish, but it had certain compensations. If Chantal were to die – a possibility that he found he could contemplate with profound satisfaction – and to die unwed, it would be his father who would fall heir to her estate. Undoubtedly something could be made of that. The earl was ignorant of his ingenious son's latest exploit, but he could not deny complicity in the earlier attempt to coerce his hapless ward into marriage. It should not be too difficult to bring pressure to bear on him. He should make over Chantal's fortune to his younger son. It would make a comfortable portion. No need to trouble one's head about sharing with brother Richard, either. Hilsborough would be quite sufficient for *him.* The more he thought of it, the lower the brandy sank in the bottle, the better he liked the scheme. Now, how to encompass his cousin's death without being brought to book for it?

Once again he regretted the premature dismissal of Perkis, who would doubtless have undertaken the task for a sufficient fee. But a little consideration convinced him that this time he must do the job himself. To be employing an underling would lay him open to blackmail for the rest of his life, and he had no intention of squandering Chantal's money in *that* wasteful fashion. He knew a good deal about blackmail, as both Rab and Perkis would have testified. There was no end to it.

He refilled his glass and turned his attention to more detailed planning. The method was soon decided. He was a good shot; and shooting could be carried out at long range and so allowed more time for escape than strangling or stabbing. It might even be attributed to accident, however suspicious one or two people might be. Since Perkis had reported fully on all that could be discovered about the daily life of Dorne, he already knew that Chantal and Dominic were accustomed to ride together each morning and usually without a groom. If he could conceal himself somewhere within range, that seemed to him the ideal opportunity. Merriden would be far too concerned with a dead or dying girl to set off in pursuit, even if he noticed the marksman's stealthy withdrawal. Best wait another day or two until the signs of his recent punishment had faded, since he had no wish to draw attention to himself. Even the horse that he would need to make good his escape must be just a decent hack, though once he had achieved a reasonable distance from the scene of his crime it would be quite a different story. He began to amuse himself by inventing alibis. He had been in Edinburgh; in Glasgow; on the

Berwick road. People were always vague about dates and times. You could persuade them to agree to anything, so your own statement was sufficiently convincing.

Chantal and Dominic rode out on that fair August morning in the happiest of moods. Dominic, having dutifully obeyed Aunt Celia's behest to inform his mama – and, incidentally, his father, too – of his proposed nuptials, they had, by the previous day's mail, received a letter so crammed with approval and pleasure that even the haughtiest bride might well have been satisfied. Chantal had been overwhelmed.

They talked happily of their plans, for the Marquess and his wife were to pay a short visit to the borders and would follow shortly upon the heels of the letter. Dominic thought that his father might be the best person to open negotiations with Lord Hilsborough, since he still did not trust himself to approach that peer with even a semblance of courtesy. They raced Pegeen against Rusty and then took them down to the water's edge and frolicked through the shallows, a game which the horses seemed to enjoy as much as their riders, and were quite unaware of the watcher concealed among the low huddle of rocks.

It was not the first time that the Honourable Giffard had watched them, and he felt safe enough in the sad coloured jacket and breeches that he had adopted as most likely to blend with the scenery. But this morning the pair seemed to be possessed of the devil. Whenever they came within range of his place of concealment, Merriden was between him and the girl. Not that he would have had the least objection to taking a shot at the fellow, but his plans did not allow for a second shot. Escape, and not re-loading would be his aim, once he had been granted an uninterrupted sight of dear Cousin Chantal.

There they were, cantering away from him along the water's edge. Annoyance mounted. This was already the third early morning visit that he had paid to the beach, and sooner or later someone was going to notice him and ask awkward questions. That group of low rocks to the north west would give him a better field of fire if he could reach them before the riders turned and saw him. But he would have to be very quick.

He began to run. Encumbered by the gun it was not so easy as he had thought. The riders had galloped gaily on firm-packed sand, but here it was loose stuff that dragged at his feet and slowed him down dangerously. He struggled on, gasping for breath. He *must* reach the shelter of the rocks before the riders turned and recognised him.

And then, suddenly, he could run no more. It was as though he had stepped into a soft sandy pit. It took him above the knees, and the more he struggled to free himself the deeper he sank. He tried, at first, to hold the gun above his head, fearful lest the clogging sand should get into the mechanism and so foil his purpose, but in a very few minutes fear for his own safety swamped every other consideration and he flung it from him. It landed on the rocks that had been his goal, but by some chance it did not go off. Had it done so, it might have saved his life, for Dominic and Chantal, who were watching the fishing boats coming into the bay, would have heard the shot. As it was, by the time they turned the horses it was already too late. He was engulfed to his shoulders and there was nothing that anyone could do.

Dominic hurried Chantal away. In one swift glance he had recognised the latest victim of the quicksands, even though the features were contorted by terror. He hoped that Chantal had not. Whatever the fellow had done, this was a shocking end, and one that a man would scarcely wish on his worst enemy. He hoped the girl need never know exactly how her cousin had met his fate. He said only that someone was in trouble in the quicksand and that he must go to bring help. She was to go back to Dorne and await him there.

This time she did not protest about his arbitrary dealings. She went quietly, soberly. Instinct, rather than actual recognition, had told her who the man was. None of the local people would ever have ventured in that dangerous vicinity. And she had distinctly seen a gun lying on the rocks. It *might* have been a fowler after wild duck, though it was early in the season for that, and, surely, the wrong time of day. She wondered if the man had been after larger game. She climbed slowly up to the turret room at the very top of the castle and watched from afar the activities of the men with planks and ladders laid on the quaking surface of the sand. As she had guessed, it was too late. Presently the attempts were abandoned. The would-be rescuers gathered in a knot on the foreshore. Someone gestured in the direction of the rocks – she was told later that these could be approached by sea as the tide rose

– and then they slowly dispersed.

It was some time before Dominic came home. She saw him from her look-out point and came down to the castle beach to greet him. He shook his lead gravely.

'Too late to be of help. Once one is in deep, it is very quick.'

She hesitated only briefly. Then she said quietly, 'Cousin Giffard?'

So she *had* seen. As well, perhaps. The men had told him that there was no hope of recovering the body, not without putting further lives at risk. Someone had brought the gun in, too, and Dominic could think of only one reason why a man should walk on a lonely beach with a gun loaded with ball. That discovery had effectually effaced any pity he might have felt for the dead man, though he still hoped that Chantal might be spared the knowledge of her cousin's intent.

She was silent for a moment or two. Then she looked at him, clear-eyed.

'I cannot grieve. Nor will I pretend to. But he is gone and can do us no further harm. Can we spare his father the full knowledge of his villainy? That gun, for instance. Can it be identified at his?'

So she had guessed the whole – or at least come pretty near the truth.

'Yes,' he admitted. 'It had his initials carved on the stock. But I took the precaution of unloading it before I handed it over to the bailie. Also of telling him that the victim was known to me. I trust that we may be able to pass the business off as accident – which, indeed, it was. It will be assumed that he was wild fowling. A bit early for it, but after all one may shoot gulls at any season.'

She nodded and left him to tell Oliver of the morning's events. She did not again refer to the matter but she was very quiet all day. Dominic coaxed her out into the garden after dinner and presently, his arm about her shoulders, asked gently what was troubling her.

'Not the business of your cousin, is it? I promise you that we shall brush through that without any difficulty. There will be no scandal to distress his relatives or to cast a slur upon your father's name.'

'In a way that *is* the trouble,' she admitted, her tone unusually subdued. 'I have been thinking. The same blood runs in my veins. Villain or not, we are both Delaneys. And I am well aware that I was much criticised by sober persons for my wild ways. How if that bad blood were to come out in me?'

His voice, in the darkness, sounded a little amused. 'My dear girl! Don't you think you are being a little fanciful? It is not *so* close a relationship. One of your grandfathers and one of your cousin's were brothers. That is all. His wickedness may well have come to him from the maternal side, or as Oliver said, he may be a throw-back to some distant ancestor, though for my part I would suggest that much of it derives from being thoroughly spoilt as a child, so that he could not endure to be thwarted.'

She sounded a little happier as she said shyly, 'So you do not think there is any danger that our children may inherit evil tendencies? That you ought, perhaps, to consider again before you marry me.'

She was perfectly serious about it, but he could not help laughing a little though his smile was very tender as he said, 'What! And disappoint Mama when she is so happy over the result of her innocent scheming to throw us together? She knew from the outset, she declares, that we were meant for each other. And Oliver – who says he never credited me with such good sense and who is insisting that we spend our winters at Merriden with him because you expressed a liking for the place. You would not have me upset all these happy plans by announcing that I had changed my mind and decided that after all you would not *do!* As for our children – they are quite as likely to inherit a fair share of deviltry from the Merriden side. Neither Oliver nor I were precisely angels! As for thinking again' – he put a masterful hand under her chin and tilted her face to his. He kissed her gently, thoughtfully, and against her lips he murmured, 'I can think only of making you wholly mine just as soon as it can be done. Shall we be married here? You love the place, I know. Or would you prefer the chapel at Merriden? It shall be just as you wish. But soon, my darling, I beg of you. For I shall not really believe my good fortune until we have exchanged the vows that will make us one till the end of time.'

The publishers hope that this book has given you enjoyable reading. Large Print Books are especially designed to be as easy to see and hold as possible. If you wish a complete list of our books please ask at your local library or write directly to:

Dales Large Print Books
Magna House, Long Preston,
Skipton, North Yorkshire.
BD23 4ND

This Large Print Book, for people
who cannot read normal print,
is published under the auspices of

THE ULVERSCROFT FOUNDATION

... we hope you have enjoyed this book.
Please think for a moment about those
who have worse eyesight than you ...
and are unable to even read or enjoy
Large Print without great difficulty.

You can help them by sending a
donation, large or small, to:

The Ulverscroft Foundation,
1, The Green, Bradgate Road,
Anstey, Leicestershire, LE7 7FU,
England.
or request a copy of our brochure for
more details.

The Foundation will use all donations
to assist those people who are visually
impaired and need special attention
with medical research, diagnosis
and treatment.

Thank you very much for your help.